H(A)P P Y

Nicola Barker

WILLIAM HEINEMANN: LONDON

1 3 5 7 9 10 8 6 4 2

William Heinemann
20 Vauxhall Bridge Road
London SW1V 2SA

William Heinemann is part of the Penguin Random House
group of companies whose addresses can be found at
global.penguinrandomhouse.com.

 Penguin
Random House
UK

First published by William Heinemann in 2017

www.penguin.co.uk

A CIP catalogue record for this book is available
from the British Library.

ISBN 9781785151149

Book design by Lindsay Nash

Printed and bound by C&C Offset Printing Co., Ltd., China

Penguin Random House is committed to a sustainable future for
our business, our readers and our planet. This book is made from
Forest Stewardship Council® certified paper.

H(A)PPY

Also by Nicola Barker

For Stefan Towler – who painted his way into
one book, then wrote his way into another

Author's note

Although by no means essential, this novel is best enjoyed in conjunction with *Agustín Barrios: The Complete Historical Guitar Recordings 1913–1942*.

In front, a corral of bamboo and two house palms. Mangoré presents himself with feathers. An anachronism. Something for children. His costume goes with the bamboo, but not with the guitar.

The reception by the public is cold and silent, with ironic comments: 'horrendous', 'shocking', 'he's on marijuana' etc.

The Indian sits, strokes his instrument in a strangely smooth manner and begins. The program does not seem to be in agreement with the situation – it indicates the Indian feels he is a musician, and that he wants to give the best he can, but my God! That savage wants to play Bach, Beethoven, Mozart, Chopin on the guitar! It seems a sacrilege. We expect a disaster, a fatal musical calamity.

He plays a Serenata Morisca of his own composition. On the mark. Another of his compositions, andante and allegretto. Notable. A Chilean dance…

The guitar becomes a piano, violin, flute, mandolin, drum. There is nothing that this man can't do on the guitar. At times it seems the guitar plays itself…

The applause grows, and increases with each piece until at the end of the performance the public is shouting 'encore' to which he replies 'thank you', simply 'thank you'.

—UNKNOWN CRITIC WRITING ABOUT THE GUITARIST
AND COMPOSER AGUSTÍN BARRIOS, AKA CHIEF NITSUGA
MANGORE, IN THE *Nuestro Diario*, GUATEMALA, 1933

Indeed, man wishes to be happy even when he so lives as to make happiness impossible.

SAINT AUGUSTINE, *City of God* (AD 476)

Happiness is brief.
It will not stay.
God batters at its sails.

EURIPIDES, *Orestes* (408 BC)

1
The New Path.

After they banded together and saved us from the Floods and the Fires and the Plagues and the Death Cults, the Altruistic Powers actively discouraged The Young from thinking about God. We walked a new path. They called it The New Path. They called it A Path of Light. And The Young were taught various, simple techniques that allowed them to feel at peace. We moved Beyond God. We were taught to celebrate This Moment. And our chemicals were balanced.

We were perfected. We were given just enough choices to make us feel as though we were free, but not so many that our minds (our still-fragile intellects) became overloaded. Doubt ended. The Information Stream was purified. Before, there was filth and it corrupted us. After, there was freshness. There was the smell of newly cut grass. Everything shone. They made us feel innocent again. No – *no*. They made us Innocent again.

We are Innocent. We are Clean and Unencumbered. Every new day, every new dawn, every new hour, every new minute, we are released once more from the tight bonds of History (the Manacles of The Past). We are constantly starting over and over from scratch. Right here! Right now! A new beginning. A New World. Everything is possible. We are reborn.

I am told that at one time (when there was recorded time – which is apparently a flawed religious concept) everything worked until a certain number was reached and then everything stopped working because nothing could cope with the magnitude of The Number. It was a finite number. All numbers were finite then. Vital resources kept running out and people suffered. Because of numbers. Just numbers. But now numbers are infinite and everything has been mapped and nothing is unknown. Nothing can run out – even life. We are eternal. And we always have enough. Just enough. We do not crave more than enough. We are content. We are In Balance. And we work hard – but never too hard – to stay In Balance. This goal is what fires us, what drives us. We are not encouraged to question how or why – although we are not discouraged from questioning, either. We just accept that the past was The Past. We live Now. We live In Light. And when darkness threatens (darkness? Can there ever truly be darkness again?) they simply adjust the chemicals. They just...*know*.

The chemicals enter us in a multitude of ways. Our environments are sensitive. Our environments are cooperative. Everything is Whole. We are total, universal, all-integrated. We are In Balance. We work (but never struggle) to stay In Balance. And everything functions perfectly. So we no longer have to worry.

Sometimes – while we sleep, as we gently dream – they remind us of how it used to be so that we appreciate how good things are now. Now that we are Free From Desire. And we are H(A)PPY to be reminded of this because it reinforces our sense of peacefulness, of calm, of conformity, of equilibrium. They tell us about the lies of The Past. Of how The Young were told that they needed to rebel against the norm in order to feel Whole. That creativity is dependent on struggle and suffering. Of how true happiness could only be felt if we completely abandoned the self to God, or, at the other extreme (The Past was full of such contradictions), of how true happiness was always contingent upon another person or creature's suffering and pain. That it was somehow 'comparative' or 'competitive'.

Lies. All lies.

When I say 'they tell us' I actually mean 'we tell us'. Because nothing is above us. Nothing is below us. We are In Balance. That is how The System was tooled. We work to stay In Balance. Each of us contributes in our own special way to this goal. I am principally a musician. This is my talent. But I do not focus exclusively on music. Nothing is ever exclusive here. To be exclusive is to exclude. And nothing is excluded. I give my time and my attention and my energy to many causes, to many occupations. I am open. I am humble. I am appreciative. I am grounded.

We have a graph – we call it The Graph – and it shows us how In Balance we are: as a person (our physical and mental health), as a small community (a community of skills, a community of friends, a community of consumers, a community of thought) and as a broader society – as a race, as a planet, as a galaxy. Many graphs, one Graph.

There is a satisfaction – a deep satisfaction – in remaining neatly within the parameters of our various graphs. In keeping things even. And we all strive (but not too hard) for that. Because it makes us H(A)PPY: just to contribute, to be utterly aware, utterly informed, utterly sensitive. Utterly open to everything.

It makes us H(A)PPY...

H(A)PPY

H(A)PPY

But why is that happening?

H(A)PPY

Why? Why does the A persist on disambiguating? On parenthesising?

And why am I talking? What am I doing? Why am I rehearsing this?

Where is the need?

H(A)PPY

H(A)PPY

How curious...
How perplexing.
A malfunction?
A blip?
A kink?
But where...?

Ah. That jangling, sweet melody. Remember?
And the child.

If it started – although I cannot describe 'it', I cannot comprehend 'it', just sense 'it', just suspect 'it' (imagine a mist of condensation on your skin which you are unaware of until a light breeze lightly gusts against your cheek), yes, if it started – this odd disambiguation, this slight discombobulation, this blip – then it started with the child – a little girl – there was, yes – when I think back – if I recall correctly – and I can't seem to get her... she keeps stealing into my mind. And she is accompanied by a strange melody. A sweet, jangling waltz. Performed on the guitar. But it's being played on metal strings. It reverberates most curiously. She is small and dark, with burning eyes and a wary smile; and my Sensor tells me that she is nine years of age and that she lived – many years ago, when there was still age – in what was once the Southern Americas. I discovered her on

The Information Stream in the margins of an article about a Paraguayan luthier who specialised in acoustic cutaways (I have been pondering the virtues of the cutaway of late). This luthier also happened to own a precious guitar – although not a cutaway. I idly followed the link.

It was strange (yes, strange) that I should be looking at an article about a precious guitar (although I am a guitarist and I play and tool guitars), because – to all intents and purposes – guitars are all precious now (and all valueless, and all the same, and all perfected, and all readily available to anyone who might feel in need of one). So it was strange that I should find myself searching The Past for information about any other kind of guitar than the kind I have which is a perfectly wonderful kind of guitar, a guitar that I am truly and completely and utterly con... con... H(A)PPY with.

H(A)PPY

And this precious guitar was anything but perfect. It was imperfect! It was a traditional, wooden guitar; pear-shaped. I focused in on the picture so intensely that the image became grainy (this was still a time when images became grainy, a time of discord, of mischief, of fracture and of pixellation. A time without True Clarity. A time of blurred edges).

This guitar – ah, this guitar – was precious not because of any inherently good qualities, but because it once belonged to a famous guitarist. It had metal strings – not gut strings. And it had tiny beads made from a kind of vulcanised rubber through which each of the treble strings had been painstakingly threaded and then positioned so as to remain flush with the bridge. These were dampers. Yes, dampers. To reduce the metallic rumble. The vibration. A compromise of sorts. A creative compromise, a curious compromise. The guitar – this patently compromised instrument – made no real sense to me. As a luthier. As a player. An acoustic guitar but with ugly metal strings at a point in History – yes, my Sensor promptly confirmed this for me – when gut strings were the only truly acceptable devices for play. This was before the electric guitar. This was before the Age of Blare, of Wah-Wah, of Rock. The 'precious' guitar was a curious anomaly. A puzzle. It sat unsteadily (1920? 1925?) – it teetered – at the end of the Past and the start of the Future (which was also a kind of past). It existed at a tipping point. At the birth of Dissonance. At the death of Harmony. It was an imperfect instrument. An anachronism. A curiosity. A puzzle. Yes, I'll say it again: a puzzle. And because I am a luthier I habitually engage with these puzzles, I struggle with them (although I do not war with them or battle with them, and I do not embrace them, either, I do not search them out, because where is the need when the solutions are ever-present, when every riddle has been finally and definitively solved?). But I found myself staring at this guitar's imperfections and wondering. I am not sure what I was wondering. There was simply a space, a wordlessness, an itch.

Yes, an itch.

I suppose I may've wondered who could have owned this imperfect object which – even in the history of guitars, of

7

guitar-making – made no real sense. Who might've owned this chaotic instrument? This clumsy, silly, senseless instrument?

And then I suddenly saw the girl, the brown-eyed child, standing there, in the margins. On the edge of a badly torn clipping. She was holding a doll, swaddled in a blanket. There she was. Just a girl.

But why should I care? We – The Young – utterly reject (my language is too harsh here, imagine a calmer version of this phrase, a more dispassionate version, if you will), we *disavow* the idea of fame and all that this titular 'garland' of The Past implies. Even the word. We even reject the word *fame* – a hot word. A steaming word. A word that condenses and then rots. A dangerous word. We abhor 'personality'. We eschew difference. And The Sensor – because we ask it to, because it needs to – actively refuses to acknowledge (and thereby credit) prominent individuals – 'famous' individuals – from the Cruel Rack of History. From the chaotic Then. From that dark and damp and foggy time before the serene purity of Now.

Because Now all creatures are equal. That is our Philosophy. No one may be raised above. So The Sensor – because we want it to, because we need it to, because we ask it to – helpfully breaks these once-lauded individuals down into their component parts. It deconstructs them. They are accorded mere numbers. They are not credited with names, because names generate a kind of tiny, psychological implosion, a connection, a dangerous synergy that bounces between the letters and the information and the image and the meaning.

This guitarist was Paraguayan and his number is 91.51.9.81. 81.1.2.

Sorry.

But...yes...then there she suddenly was, the child, this haunting girl, and because she was on the margins of the page – the page about the precious guitar – I could not access the full story (I could not ably guide my Sensor – where might I direct it? How? When there were no other clues?), even though I tried. I tried hard. I tried several times. I almost became...I don't know...I almost became *frustrated*.

Breathe. Breathe.

Push it away, Mira A. This moment. This feeling. This frustration. Frustration is nothing more than an unhealthy burgeoning of the rampant Ego. Frustration is entitlement. Frustration is arrogance. Check The Graph. Is it pinkening? Is it?
Oh just let it pass, Mira A. Inhale. Exhale.
Forgive yourself. Forget yourself.
That's right. Yes. That's better...
Well done.
Good.
Phew!

But still, still, there was something so...so old, so...so *intriguing* about that small child's dark eyes. They haunted me. Of course I tried to receive the information – as little as I had – and then let it go. The way we have been taught to.

But I found it hard to let go. I don't understand why. Perhaps there was a blip, a kink. Yes. I think my chemicals must have become unbalanced. It's very strange. I will ask for help. Oh. Somebody has already noticed. On The Graph. How lovely. There is help. Help is already here.

2
Help!

He was a Full Neuter and his name was Kite. His Identifier has a little logo of a cheerful green kite with a long, dancing tail weighted down by a series of pretty, red bows. But for some reason I thought of the hunting bird. I secretly wished that his logo was of a hunting bird.

'Too masculine.' He smiled, noting that my Sensor had called up information about the hunting bird.

'Of course.' I smiled. Of course.

Kite checked my chemicals. He made a couple of tiny adjustments. He asked about my given name, Mira A, which I am told is the name of a star – a giant, red star – and also means 'boundless' in one of the many old languages from The Past. Then he asked about my guitar (my logo is a simplified version of 41.51.91.21.51.8.3.9.41–41.5.2's *Musical Instruments*; an abstract image in greys and blues and browns of two, stringed instruments, somehow conjoined, facing each other, one – the most dominant – a guitar, the other possibly a cello or a violin, each separate but somehow a part of the other).

Because I sensed that he liked music and that it would make him H(A)PPY – and therefore more productive –

I improvised Kite a short piece on my guitar which I spontaneously called 'Watching the Dawn Break on the New Delta'.

Kite was astonished at how nimbly my fingers plucked away at the guitar strings. It made him H(A)PPY to watch this and to listen. Yes, it did make him H(A)PPY. H(A)PPY and refreshed. Although he was already perfectly H(A)PPY. Kite is In Balance.

'That rapid movement with your right hand,' he murmured, once I'd finished. 'A tremolo?'

I nodded.

And then, just to be on the safe side, I quickly told Kite about the little girl who I had seen on the margins (although of course I didn't *need* to tell Kite anything. Kite already has open access on The Stream to all my thoughts and my movements and my transactions). Kite was, nevertheless, quite surprised that anything marginal should be in focus. He aimed a tiny laser into my right eye and peered around inside for a few moments, wondering aloud whether there might be something slightly off-kilter in my Oracular Devices. He scratched his head. He made a mental note of it. I told him that I had been idly looking at an article about a precious guitar and that I didn't entirely understand why my Sensor had called it up in the first place.

'You must've asked it to,' he said, matter-of-factly, then added, without any prompting, 'I like most stringed instruments, but not the violin. For some reason I find the sound of violins rather sad and unsettling. Too emotional. Even jigs. Even jigs make me feel uneasy – as if the riotous surface of celebration masks something underneath, some kind of . . . of emptiness or . . . or inadequacy.'

He shuddered when he used these words: unsettling – emptiness – inadequacy. Kite is so sensitive that the words scratch up against the smooth surface of his calm psyche and pucker it; disarrange it.

'But don't you think there might be a special kind of sadness that is almost a form of happiness?' I mused. For some inexplicable reason (and as Kite so astutely observed slightly earlier in our exchange) I have been thinking a great deal about the tremolo of late – those wavering high notes: so sweet, so sad. I have a powerful urge to play those notes, although without the familiar fixed-chord positions so typical of the classical and the flamenco traditions (using an independent melodic line instead). This is difficult. It means great stretches of the left hand. It's challenging and uncomfortable. Hence my interest in the cutaway guitar. The cutaway provides much greater flexibility to individuals with smaller hands and shorter fingers.

'Are you referring to the state of melancholy, perhaps?' Kite hazarded a quick guess.

'Ah. Yes. Melancholy.' I nodded. 'Isn't there often a bright azure tinge of happiness to be found glinting away quietly inside the deep shadows of its murky-grey waters?'

'By my reckoning, that "special" kind of happiness sounds suspiciously like an EOE.' He chuckled. 'An unproductive form of self-indulgence.'

(Kite is obviously very wise. I can see him receiving information and then only holding on to it just as long as he absolutely needs to, but no longer. He doesn't grasp on to it. He just receives it and then pushes it away. He gives it away. He is enviably Non-Attached.)

'It permeates music.' I shrugged, almost resigned. 'It lives in the minor keys.'

Kite called something up on his Sensor. 'Your star oscillates,' he muttered, leaving a quick, mental note about this in his brand-new Mira A file.

'My...?'

'Mira A, your star, the star you are named after, it oscillates. Sometimes it is visible from our planet, from Mother Earth, but at other times it vanishes from view. And there is a Mira B. Another star. A sister star. A less well-formed star.'

'I wonder if I'll feel still more H(A)PPY – still more complete – when I finally transition into a Full Neuter...' I pondered. 'Like you.'

I gazed up at him, admiringly.

'False aspiration.' He smiled. 'Happy is Happy is Happy.' Then he flipped on the laser and peered into my right eye again and made another mental note of something. I suppose I could easily call it up on my Information Stream if I really wanted to know what it was. But I trust Kite completely. So I don't care.

I asked Kite how long he had been in My Orbit. I haven't encountered Kite before. Kite began to answer me and then I interrupted him to ask if he would consider joining my Community of Friends. Kite was H(A)PPY to oblige me, although he said that he never refused friendship and that he considered the whole world to be his Community.
Kite is so Well Balanced.

Now I come to think of it, I somewhat regret not waiting to hear Kite's answer to my question about how long he had been in My Orbit. I would've liked to find out the answer.

I suppose it was rather rude of me to interrupt him like that. Of course I could call up this information on my Stream if I wanted to, but if I do that then Kite will automatically be informed and I don't want to distract him (or anyone else) with my excessive – even inappropriate – levels of interest. I need to turn these impulses inwards: first, to the self, then, to the Community, and finally, to The Graph.

Balance.

I regret my rudeness. I regret it, then I push it away. We cannot live in regret, that would be self-defeating. We can only live in This Moment.

Kite is so friendly. He is so Well Balanced. He's great. I really need to spend more time around positive people like Kite. But I also need to counter this desire with a sense of calm resignation, of deep renunciation and of effortless self-control.

For your information:

EOE

An EOE is an Excess of Emotion. To stay In Balance we must avoid Excesses of Emotion. All excesses. Any excess. Extremes are deeply unproductive. They are dangerous. Even the word 'dangerous' is potentially dangerous – and only to be employed with immense self-awareness and caution – because it is an extreme word and words carry suggestions the way the wind carries pollen and leaves and dust particles. And music. And Kites.

I am an oscillating star.

Who is Mira B?

Gosh!
I recently discovered…

There is a way of sidestepping the gaze of The Information Stream. I have only recently found this out. By staring into bright light. I came upon this information purely by accident. And I asked that question (the one you just read) – Who is Mira B? – staring into bright light. Blinding light. I am staring into bright light as I think this. Of course if I stare into blinding light too often it will become apparent on The Graph as A-Typical Behaviour. And I do not want to negatively affect The Graph. Already I can see that my numbers are higher than they should be. There is a purpling effect at the edge of the Colourmap. I must be open. I must be transparent. I must walk a Path of Light instead of being... of slipping... of becoming... I must not... I must avoid this strange urge to be Blinded By The Light.

Blinded By...

Blinded By The...

Why is that phrase capitalised on my Information Stream?
Like a song title?
How perplexing!
Of course I shouldn't want anything too much. That's the secret. That's the key. I should not strain. I need to let these thoughts go and Move On. I am Free From Desire.
I am H A P P Y.
Yes. Yes. I am H (A) P P Y.

H(A)P P Y

H(A)P P Y

I am In Balance.

Oh why does the A keep on disambiguating?
The A in H (A) P P Y?

Why does it keep on parenthesising like that?

What can it possibly mean?

3
The Farm.

All our fabrics are intelligent now. We grow them in laboratories. Our fabrics are self-cleaning and self-maintaining and they interact with our bodies to gauge things like size, density and temperature according to the specifics of the conditions in which we find ourselves. Our fabrics – our shoes – are alive. They are sensitive and so we – The Young – are sensitive to them. Appreciative of them. In situations of stress or duress or jeopardy our clothes will modify to protect us. They are fully breathable. They will change colour on request. We can wear any style or pattern that we choose, but mostly we choose to wear plain, loose, non-gendered styles and the colour white because we are The Young and we are Clean and we try not to complicate things too much by engaging The Ego in mundane or insignificant day-to-day decisions. Choice, fashion etc. are the pointless and outmoded preoccupations of The Past. And colour often represents The Ego. The Ego and difference. So we can choose to wear whatever we like, but we always choose to wear white, because it best expresses how calm we are, and how free we are, and how whole we are and how H(A)PPY we are.

H (A) P P Y

I really, really wish it would stop doing that.

Separating.
Oscillating.

And yet even though our fabrics are sentient, and our food is carefully prepared in laboratories where levels of power and water and waste etc. are all minutely controlled – we eschew the old Capitalist Modes of Production and quietly consider them the greatest human evil (please note that I employ this provocative word with a combination of calm and regret and disquiet), The Young still choose to spend time In Nature, at regular intervals, to keep in touch with our dear Mother, Earth. Mother Earth is our sustainer, our source, our root, and we love her. When we touch Mother Earth something fundamental is stimulated within us and we feel an intense sensation of Actuality and Belonging. Because we live in The System it is sometimes easy to forget that at the root of everything is Mother Earth who sustains us. We live in The System but we must look behind it, the way a child in The Past might watch a puppet show and then – once the performance is over – run to the back of the box and lift up the curtain to squint into the darkness at the hunched and mysterious (and no doubt heavily perspiring) figure of the puppeteer.

In The Past our ancestors forgot to love (and love is a strong word, a dangerous word, a word The Young are discouraged from using if any other word will suffice) Mother Earth. They created Gods in their own image and worshipped these images instead of Mother Earth. They told themselves that the creator of the universe had chosen *them* and made *them* rulers over all things – all the plants and the animals, all Mother Earth's many riches and resources. Soon they invented their demi-gods of Growth and Progress. They forgot that Mother Earth sustained them freely. They were arrogant and self-serving. Their philosophies were both physically and intellectually flawed. They worshipped the number. They became an unsustainable parasite on Mother Earth. They stole from Mother Earth. They abused her and all her many glories. Their ignorance and vanity were insupportable. They forgot how to feel gratitude. They forgot how to see, how to empathise, how to reason.

Yes. Oh yes. That is who we once were. The Young must never, ever allow themselves to ignore what has brought them here. The Young must never, ever forget the debt that they owe to Mother Earth. Insofar as it is helpful and fruitful, The Young must feel a measure of shame and embarrassment (even consternation, even disgruntlement, even astonishment) at the chaos and destruction their own race has unleashed against Mother Earth. Shame. Embarrassment. Sharp words. Dangerous words. And, as such, it is only appropriate that The Young should embrace them for a moment – a brief moment – then push them away and move on. It is a lesson. It is why we live by The Graph. We cannot be self-serving. We cannot be individual. We are one consciousness fractured into a multitude of forms. We cleave to what is good and, still more importantly, what is feasible. Our survival is dependent upon our unity. We must be dispassionate. The System is our unity. The System is our dispassion.

But The System is not our God.
We are our own Gods.

The farm … The farm … Oh, yes.

I am currently on a farm tending to a herd of cows. Lorca, who I am working alongside, has been encouraging me to pat their flanks as we lead them to milking. Lorca is a *masseuse*. She specialises in touch. I – in turn – encourage Lorca to listen to the heavy, panting breath of the cows, and the chop and thud and rhythm of their hooves against different surfaces. We especially enjoy the sound the jets of warm milk make against the side of the steel pail when we stretch out our tentative hands to gently squeeze their soft and wonderfully pendulous nipples.

Such an extraordinary thought: that our ancestors once drank this strange, warm liquid and felt themselves to be sustained by it, even though many of them lacked the correct enzymes to digest it properly. We are naturally overwhelmed by the cow's rich, heady smell, its stolid unknowingness, its immense mass, its easy heaviness. And the way that their patient flanks steam so gloriously in the cold, morning air. At first I was afraid of the herd, but the cows are not dangerous to us. They are simulacra (cows were viral minefields in The Past, and when farmed industrially were contributors to the depletion of Mother Earth's precious Ozone Layer), but they are utterly lifelike. And for every Human there are three Neuro-Mechanicals, ensuring that The Young are always kept safe from harm – even though there *is* no prospect of harm – because that's how very precious we are – to each other, to the world. I say precious, but of course we are not precious at all. We must not think in that way. We must always remain humble. We must strive (but not too hard, never *too* hard) to be Ego-less. Our value is, of course, purely negligible and entirely contingent upon the tiny mark we make in the immense pattern of The Whole. In a time of True Clarity, we are that oft-derided pixellated dot. That is all. And we must never forget it. The Young are an Impressionistic Masterpiece, a perfect Art Form, a gloriously Open Composition. But Mira A? Who is she? Mira A is just a small, individuated brush stroke. A tiny, insignificant splash within a giant, glowing canvas of Light.

I am H(A)PPY with that.

H(A)PPY.

I am…

Oscillating.

Move on, Mira A. Just let it pass.
Inhale. Exhale.
Forgive yourself. Forget yourself.
That's right. Yes. Yes. That's better.

It is always good to have a short break from The Sensor, although we can never really have a break from The Sensor, just the idea of a break, just the semblance of a break. The break is supplied and managed and supervised by The Sensor to give us a break from The Sensor. It is almost like experiencing pangs of thirst while swimming in a bottomless ocean of water.

The irony of this situation is by no means lost on us. The Young have a well-developed sense of humour. It is necessary. We are wry, but we are accepting. We are the inheritors of something almost destroyed, something virtually ruined, something tragically despoiled and bruised and limping, but we will not – no, we will not – allow this tragedy to undermine our hopefulness, or our determination to work hard to improve, piece by piece, inch by inch, increment by tiny increment, this brave and clever planet that we love so dearly. Our Mother. Earth.

Sometimes, on the farm, I gaze into the 'sun' and think illicit thoughts (I am doing just that as I think this). I am not even entirely sure what these thoughts are, what they amount to – they are so quick, so fleeting – but it feels good to release them – to unburden myself of them. Afterwards my mind vibrates like a metal string.

The image of a dog, emerging from a river, standing on the green bank, pressing its four paws into the soft soil, securing itself, and then *shaking* its fur free of any excess moisture – just *shaking* itself – is how I best like to conceptualise this process.

An unburdening.

I will not allow myself to regret this strange weakness, because regret is counterproductive. I will just allow these thoughts to form, ponder them for a moment (the way one might ponder a healing mosquito bite on the skin of a smooth arm) and then calmly push them away. I will not allow these unhelpful formulations to compromise my time on the farm. The Graph at the farm is very stable. I observed this to Lorca after the dawn milking and she said, 'I believe that's a pun.'

I did not know what a pun was, so she explained it to me. A pun is a kind of internal joke connected to language use. Farm/stable. That was the pun.

Pun.

How did I not know that?

Surely I knew that?

Oscillating.

I enjoy being around Lorca. She often massages my hands and my feet. I value her touch. There is no awkwardness between us. The Young are unafraid of intimacy. Because everything is Known. Everything is Open. Nothing is hidden. And we are no longer sexually driven. There is no need. There is no urge. No desperation. Just calm. We are untroubled. We are Free From Desire. Over time our bodies have become smoother. Our reproductive organs have shrunk and become neutral. Some of The Young choose to advance this process chemically if it is considered appropriate by The Graph. If it is considered better for them to do so. Others are encouraged to wait for this to happen naturally. This is good, too. It is nice to be smooth. But we do not idealise smoothness. It shouldn't be considered a 'goal' – the 'apex' of anything – a state of 'perfection'. It is simply an evolution. Evolution is not a moral conundrum – a challenge, a dilemma. Evolution is not an emotional issue. It is a drab fact, a necessity, an inevitability. That is all. It is something natural. When a snake sheds its skin it does not consider the skin it once had or the skin it now has. It just accepts the process and moves on. It does not dwell on these things, because it is not good to dwell on these things. It is not useful or fruitful to dwell on these things. Because The System is perfection. It was made perfect. It expresses us perfectly, and we express it perfectly. We are a Whole. So there is no need to worry, or to gnaw, or to swerve…

Ah…
Look…

As I thought *gnaw*…As I thought *swerve*…the tiny graph that calibrates my language choice pinkened, ever so slightly, and a small light flashed. It said volatile. The Graph does not approve of my choice of language. The Graph thinks I am verging on an EOE. Volatile. I call up an explanation of this word on The Sensor – *volatile* – and the *Oxford English Dictionary* tells me that my language choice was 'mercurial'. Mercurial? The dictionary tells me that to be mercurial is to be 'of lively temperament'.

For a brief second I gaze up into the 'sun' and wonder whether the planet Mercury is related to the planet Mira A. Two big, red planets, remember? Big. Boundless. Volatile. Mercurial. But Mars may always be seen, is always visible (unless it draws too close to the sun). Mira A *oscillates*. She *oscillates*.

And Mira B? What of Mira B? That strange sister planet. Does *she* oscillate?

Brief moments of volatility aside, The Graph at the farm is relatively stable. No pun intended. And that is a relief. That is a great relief. I don't want to disrupt The Graph. I don't want to be the weakest link. I want to play my part. I am so grateful to be one of The Young. I am not proud. Pride is unhealthy. I am grateful. I am honoured. And I want to do everything I can to keep The Graph strong.

All those bad feelings…

Don't push them away, Mira A. Remember: a push is almost a shove and a shove is far too aggressive.
Just turn away from them.
Just turn away.
Don't push.
Never push.

Just turn.
Gently turn.

It is surprisingly difficult to explain our loyalty to each other – as a tribe, as a Community, as a race (for who may truly understand The Young except The Young, after all? We do not crave understanding. We are without need. We are complete. We do not require constant validation). We are never encouraged to be too loyal or too devoted (to anything or anyone), to form too strong an attachment, except to The System. If one's happiness becomes too dependent upon – or too invested in – another person, then one loses the ability to control one's own destiny. And that would be unhealthy. For the individual. For the object of desire. For the group. For the society. For the race. For the planet. We are a Whole. The System is our reason. It is our answer. It is our hope. It is our strength. The System contains everything we might possibly need. It completes us. We complete it.

That is all.

That –

is –

all.

4

A New Song.

I cannot remember (although The Sensor is, of course, nudging me with information – but I choose to ignore it, I choose to dwell, just briefly, in forgetfulness) when I first began to hear The New Song. Perhaps it was on the farm. Perhaps I started to hum it under my breath on the dawn stroll with Lorca for the early milking. Yes. There is something clean and haunting about the start of the song. It is a waltz that is both strangely innocent and oddly knowing.

I call it a song, but it has grown much bigger than that. It is slowly swelling within my mind. It is a whole new repertoire – something far more complex, more convoluted, more ambitious than anything I have ever engaged with before. You might call it a mosaic – a musical mosaic. There are many parts to it. Six at the very least. Six strong voices. And each plucks and hums in a different way – resonates at a different level. There are six main instruments – but they are all the guitar.

Of course The Young are not generally encouraged to experiment with music from The Past (although they are not *dis*couraged from this practice, either. We are never bound or curtailed, we are always at liberty – we are perpetually free). We understand that all composition must, at some level, *refer* to The Past – to a particular instrument's Body of Work (for example), to Classics of the Idiom. We are – we must inevitably be, at some level, however much we might resist the notion – the Sum of Our Influences. But The Young are Clean and we are Hopeful and we are Unattached. Our music must, by necessity, reflect this freshness (my Language Graph pinkens at the word *must*, then pinkens still further at *necessity*. Too trenchant – too…ah yes – too mercurial).

The Cultural Edifices of The Past are a warped and diseased outgrowth of the Hopelessness and Corruption of History (I say this very slowly, very calmly). For how might they expect to be otherwise? They are (very calm, very slow again) spoiled and bruised by association in much the same way a ripe peach – in all its innocence, in all its purity – will be bruised and spoiled by the greedy fingers of a coarse and acquisitive hand.

There are many Art Forms that are no longer compatible with The New Path. Art is, by its very nature, an expression of Ego. Art describes the world – it is once removed from the world (it cannot be in This Moment. But The Young *live* in This Moment, so our Art must, by sheer necessity, be improvised and impermanent). That once-removedness of Art is an expression (a validation, a celebration) of a kind of difference, a kind of vanity. It is interpretation. It is embellishment. It is cynicism. It is ideology. If Art may exist among The Young, then it needs to Shine A Light on to The New Path – to bring greater dispassion, freedom and clarity (if such a thing is possible – the Path *is* Perfect, the Path *is* Freedom, the path *is* Clarity). So The Young study forms, they process archetypes (we *understand* the lie of Art – how it points to an escape. But we do not *want* to escape. Our reality is good enough. If This Moment is perfectly satisfactory, why might it require further augmentation?). When we access songs and other musical compositions from The Past we embrace them as mere skeletons. Their bones have been scraped clean. They are boiled down, just vague semblances of their former gaudy selves. Mere nuclei. Mere marks on a page. And we experiment with them. But we do not create Art for posterity. Nothing is permanent here. Nothing is embedded. Everything is in This Moment. Everything simply floats in the perpetual shelter of The Present.

Even our buildings are mutable. All structures – narrative, musical, architectural – must contain within them the capacity to be remade. There are no permanent edifices. Only The System. Only The Young. Only these two may remain indefinitely.

I have searched for the nucleus of The New Song –
Why is that capitalised? –
I have tried to uncover its clean bones so that I might work with it and make it sing again. But I cannot find it. I have searched and searched. Perhaps I should simply let it go? As we are taught to. Perhaps I should have quietly turned away by now. Because are these not the Manacles of The Past affixing themselves to me? Weighing me down? But The Graph...
The Graph is stable.
Yes. So I have crafted it from memory –

Ah, but I am getting ahead of myself. I must find the 'sun'. I must stare into the 'sun'. So that I can extrapolate a little. So that I can be truly candid.

I found the girl! There. Now you know. I found her on The Stream as I was lucid dreaming. I didn't plan it that way, although it wasn't entirely accidental. But it wasn't calculated, either. I think you might best call it almost... almost, well, a kind of H(A)PPY accident. And the music... Ah the music washes around her, with its metallic jangle, its curious sad-happiness, its odd teetering between worlds, between knowing and unknowing. Its abundant mystery. But these are very early days. There is still much to...

Oh.

The Graph has purpled.
I must've turned away from the light. Just for a second.

Breathe
Breathe

Let's just...
Try and...
Something...

Ah yes ... Did I mention that Kite visited?
Did I ... ?

How odd.
Kite's name has pinkened.
Just very slightly – ever so slightly.
And again!
But why would ... ?
I don't ...

Why would ... ?

Is it ... ?
Might it ... ?
Am I ... ?

While I'm on the subject ...

Remember that dolly? The dolly she held? The little girl? Her
dolly? Well, it wasn't a dolly. It was a baby. A tiny baby. But
the pixellation is really intense. The baby flashes in and out
of focus, very rapidly. It ... it vibrates. And when I look at the

child my eyes, as I dream, begin to flicker, quite uncontrollably. My heart pounds. And I know that there is some kind of confusion – an awful **misunderstanding**, a heavy cloud, an **obfuscation**, that is swathed around (that swaddles) all this... this apparent innocence...

A minor chord. That is how I hear it. That is how I feel it. As a minor chord.

She calls to me, this child, in a strange, scratchy waltz. *Her* song.

The subject?!
But was I even *on* the subject?

Oh shut up! Shut up!

Push it away!
Push it away, Mira A!
Don't let it...
Try not to let it be...

Breathe
Breathe

Because while The Sensor isn't...
Which conversation is this? I feel lost. How many...?
Which...?

Push it away, Mira A!
Breathe
Breathe

Because while The Sensor isn't (to use the rather unhelpful, over-simplistic and old-fashioned formulation from The Past) 'censored', there is still a whole world of information out there that is not readily available. Not quite. It is certainly present. Of course. It is existent. It is open. It is extensive – in fact it is voluminous. Almost infinite. It is not 'forbidden' or 'out of bounds' – nothing is forbidden or out of bounds to The Young: we are free – but it may still, nonetheless, only be acquired gradually, carefully, through an easy and natural progression of thoughts. And at every turn The Graph will ask the enquirer how helpful, how appropriate, how beneficial, this information is both to themselves and to The Young (because The Graph *is* The Young, after all. We are one). So, to put it simply (to break it down into its component parts), the enquirer thinks (they enquire, they ponder, they speculate) and The Sensor automatically responds. It fleshes things out or it offers tiny, factual interjections. For personal use. For simple, day-to-day decisions. But for larger, more obtuse or abstract ideas and formulations, a series of gentle, neural pathways must slowly be established (imagine cutting down a tree and then chiselling a chair from it, very quietly and patiently, slither by slither). A kind of gradual validation must take place. Because we (The Young) cannot (and should not) move from a standing start to an all-out sprint without due care and consideration. We don't ever want to risk the threat of social or psychic injury. So first there must be a slow walk, then a gentle trot, then a steady jog. The enquirer will not want to pinken The Graph by dint of asking anything too brash or too startling. The enquirer must be tentative. Modest. Helpful. Appropriate. Knowledge must be gained through a natural, cautious, gradual progression of gentle mental movements, tiny pulses. It must not jar. Because that would be unhealthy. That would be (please forgive my lurid language) *wrong*.

It is not that The Sensor or The Information Stream or The Graph or, indeed, The Young (for what are The Sensor and The Graph and The Stream if not The Young – our united consciousness, our core selves?) are against flights of fancy, *per se*, or crazy spontaneity, or bright flashes of inspiration – it's just that The Ego, the Selfish id, is often most readily and most easily expressed on a sudden whim, arbitrarily, brashly, without due care or thought. The Young need to be more wary, more intelligent, more considered.

We cannot stand guard over others (that would be

nothing short of bullying, of oppression) so we must all stand guard – first and foremost – over ourselves.

In The Past people were suddenly able to make instant connections – for a Golden Period, at least, before the onset of the Slow Epoch (when the corporations bought up and owned all seeds, all growth, all hope, all water, all clean air, all assets, all thought). During this Golden Period, The Old were completely awash with facts and non-facts. They asked a question and it was promptly answered. A fountainhead of information was released. But was the water clean? Did it quench, revive or simply deluge? Did it not often threaten to saturate and drown?

We have constrained the fountainhead. We have not stopped it. But we have inhibited it. We have redirected its flow. The Young accept that this is necessary. To be unconstrained – to expect total liberty – is not a healthy or a fruitful way to coexist. Because The Young do not believe (as The Old once did) that they have a natural right to information. Information – like all the other Old Vices (money, lust, possessions) – can be stored up – amassed – and exploited, or used to manipulate and undermine others. Information is dangerous. It is a weapon. It is explosive. Implosive. It must be handled gingerly. And it must be reliable. But who decides what is to be relied upon? Information is wanton. It is just as likely to be untrue as truthful. So we need Perspective. And The Graph provides The Young with Perspective. We can trust in it. We know that it may be depended upon. So we no longer need to worry.

We must trust The Graph because it is *us*. We must move forward gingerly, cooperatively. Because we are only strong if we are one. This sweet, fragile, *honest* organism – The Young – can only survive if it is compliant, subservient, obliging, calm, selfless, logical.

So, yes, *yes*, I have been dreaming her of late. The Graph is less sensitive to our dreams – allows greater leeway. Of course there will be a pinkening, but it is only slight. And I have discovered that I may explore the ideas that now fill my mind – that **smoulder within me** (forgive this phrase. It is wholly unnecessary. I get carried away with myself. The Graph instantly threatens an EOE) – if I transform the lucid dreams into music. So I am composing. And I find that I can compose, if I am very careful, without affecting the graph too dramatically. Kite tells me…Oh, I saw Kite again. Didn't I mention that already? I bumped into Kite at a most informative seminar about beneficial fungi. Kite tells me that The Graph automatically accommodates creativity. The Graph allows Creatives a tiny amount of extra leeway. Although The Young are all creative. It's written into our basic DNA – to evolve, to create. Because The System is, in essence, a creative entity; a truth, an aspiration, a hope, an imagining. And The Young must be creative to remain abreast of change, of variations, of threats, of nature's vagaries. So The Young are encouraged to be creative. And this is built into The Graph. If it were not, Kite says, then The Graph would be our jailer, surely?

A short pause. A nervous laugh. Was it nervous? A nervous laugh?

I should push that thought away. It is unhelpful. Although I find that the more I write the song the harder it becomes to push these thoughts away. The song is ever-present – tingling in my fingertips – and yet still it eludes me. The thoughts, though, the *thoughts*, they tumble forward, panting, like a stream of notes, a vast and indigestible symphony.

There are so many things I need to explain.
The lucid dreaming.
The story of the girl.
The song.
The second meeting with Kite.

And yet ever since I have been composing the song – The New Song – I find it difficult to think about anything else. The New Song consumes me.

Almost an EOE!
I must stop for a while. I must pause. Please forgive . . .

Consumes.
Me.

I was . . . I was . . . oh . . . oh . . . overwhelmed.

5
The Cathedral.

Kite sits me down and shines a laser into my eyes.

'You are building a Cathedral in your mind,' he says, quite matter-of-factly. 'Soon you will want to fill it with people. And then, when you have established a congregation, you will finally open it up to God.'

He turns off the laser.

Cathedral?!
God?!

I glance over towards his Graph in a blind panic. But it is void. It is blank.

'I have temporarily deactivated our Graphs,' Kite says.
What? De ... ? I gape. Mine too?

'Yours too,' he says.
It's as though Kite knows what I am thinking before I even think it. As if Kite *is* The Graph.
I gaze at him, questioningly.

'I am The Mechanic,' he explains. 'I serve The System. I fix leaks. You are leaking, Mira A. It's nothing too serious at this stage. At worst, I think we may simply be dealing with a minor endocrine fail.'

Nothing too serious?

'Is it my fault?' I ask, lifting a trembling hand to my throat.

Have I betrayed The Young? Have I betrayed *myself*?

'You've felt an itch,' he says.

'Yes. An itch. You're right.' I nod, remembering that itch. 'Is it a symptom?'

'You have constructed a narrative,' he continues.

I look slightly confused.

'Sometimes you talk to yourself.' He smiles.

'Oh.' I frown.

'I have inspected the narrative,' Kite continues, 'I have studied it carefully, in quite some detail. And it's very… its flow is, well, it's plodding – pedestrian – fluctuating – halting – occasional. It's intermittent, at best.'

'Oscillating,' I murmur.

'Narratives are not your speciality.' He glances over at me, almost pityingly.

'Music is my main… my main… preoccupation,' I stammer, with a slight shrug.

Yes. Music. That is where my talent lies.

Talent.

I glance over at The Graph but the word hasn't pinkened. There is no word.

It feels strange.

Hollow.

Cold.

Dreadful.

'Of course you will be familiar with the narrative form, *per se*,' Kite airily expands, 'you will have studied the Map of All Narratives. You will have familiarised yourself with it. You will understand the rudiments, the bare bones of all those curious narrative structures employed so often and so successfully in The Past. The narratives of family and romance and adventure, the masculine and the feminine narratives, the narratives of class, of nationalism, of capitalism, of socialism, of faith and myth and mystery, historical narratives, science fiction narratives, experimental narratives, horror narratives, literary narratives, 'reality' narratives, crime narratives... The Sensor automatically deconstructs these stories for us, so that we may fully comprehend their true meaning, their immense reach and their invidious power, their ultimately deeply conservative urge to comfort and pander and bolster and reassure. To understand them is to disable them. It's how we stay safe. By knowing. By being aware. It's how The Young remain strong and Clean. By keeping vigilant. But still, even knowing these things – as you do, as you must – narrative is not really your speciality, Mira A. Your story is only half a story. Occasional. Trite. Partial. Meandering. And, strange as this may seem, this is actually a very good thing.'

Only half a story? I am startled. Trite? Meandering? Although, even as I am startled, even as I am slightly galled by Kite's undeniably somewhat superior and patronising tone, I am also deeply relieved to hear this (it's good news, after all, positive news).

Not my 'speciality'?

'The Young do not "specialise" in anything,' I mutter, 'because that would be to exclude.'

'I've seen how you've been struggling,' he adds, ignoring my sullen interjection, 'and I've sympathised. You are falling, Mira A, but you don't even seem to grasp the fact that you *are* falling. You lack the necessary self-awareness, somehow.'

I keep glancing over towards our Graphs, every few seconds, just instinctively, and each time I am rendered almost insensible – almost speechless – by their lack of responsiveness. I feel frozen. Amputated. Yes, *yes*. Like I'm free-falling.

'You are a musician,' he says, 'you create different kinds of narratives. Subtler ones. More illusive. But they can still offer a serious threat to The System if simply left to run wild.'

'What will happen if we can't find the leak?' I ask, eyes turning again and again to the Graphs, my pulse pumping, my stomach knotting…

(Where did this awful feeling come from? This gnawing anxiety? Because there is no need… The Young… there is no need to worry because… because The Graph… because…)

'You must determine to stop telling this story,' Kite says, 'or you will poison The Graph. You will pollute The Information Stream. You will unbalance The Sensor.'

He pauses. 'You will effectively declare war on The Young.' *War?*

'But how…?' I finally whimper, flinching, almost tearful. My mind is in turmoil.

'If you are not with us, you are against us,' Kite calmly explains.

I don't know how to respond, exactly, so I slowly shake my head, indicate clumsily and stutter, 'The Graph...How did you...?'

'That isn't the issue.' Kite suddenly seems quite exasperated. 'The issue is that you are *still* telling your story. Even this – our exchange – is now gradually becoming a part of it. And I am a character in the story. I'm being co-opted, reinvented, *used*. And that's not acceptable. I don't *want* to be a character in your story, Mira A. I want to be my own character in my own story...' He pauses. 'No. I don't want to be a character at all. I just want to be myself. I just want to be in This Moment. Unconstrained. Unfettered. I want to freely submit my Ego to The Graph, to The Sensor, to The System, to The Young. But you are making this impossible for me.'

'I'm so very sorry, Kite,' I apologise, tears trickling down both cheeks, 'for compromising your freedom in this way. I like you. I admire you. I really didn't mean to.'

'You don't need to apologise,' Kite says, 'because we are friends. But you do need to stop using me in your narrative. If my character becomes too significant and the narrative becomes permanently embedded on The Information Stream then The System will become polluted. You must stop thinking about me, Mira A. You must push these thoughts away. You must tear down The Cathedral.'

'I will! I shall! I'll tear it down, Kite,' I exclaim. 'Right here. Right now.'

But even as I speak I can feel this structure – this...this 'Cathedral' as Kite calls it – arching so powerfully, so determinedly, within me. I feel its firm foundations digging into my muscle, its tall, granite walls straining against my ribs. How best might I describe this extraordinary construction, this strange, shiny new edifice? What single word might I employ? Could I call it…*desire*? Yes. Is that it? Desire? It is unquestionably an itch. A yearning. It exists in the place where my heart once beat. This great edifice. This hungry monolith. There is a smell of incense and burning candle wax. The giant candelabra are all lit, bouncing a vast kaleidoscope of light against the walls and the stained glass of the windows…

'The real danger with your narrative, so far as I can tell,' Kite says (Kite is saying), 'is that it is lazy. It is arbitrary. You are working in a world of coincidence. Of chance. You are idly playing with random details. You are forcing things together. You are forging strange connections. And you are struggling to make a kind of sense out of them. That is precisely how Great Lies originate. Remember The Past? The War of Obfuscation? The Plague of Conspiracy? This is what killed The Old. Not fact, but superstition. Not knowledge, but ignorance. The veneration of 'the urge', the 'hunch'. You believe you are being original, brilliant, brave, free, spontaneous, dynamic, innovative, nurturing, but you are not. You are walking into a blind alley and when you hit the wall instead of turning back you start tearing at the bricks. Frantically, pointlessly. Until your nails begin to snap, until your fingers bleed. *What is behind the blind alley?* you scream. *What is the mystery? What is the secret?*

'But these are empty questions. There is no secret here, no mystery, just empty speculation. This is nothing more than pure ignorance in action.'

I nod. Kite is right. I am trying to make sense out of nothing. I am trying to forge connections where there are none. I am asking questions that have no answers, but still, *still* I persist in asking them.

'The System contains everything we need, Mira A,' Kite wheedles. 'Just keep reminding yourself of that fact. Be happy! Be grateful! Because The System has been perfected. You no longer need to worry! It is infinite. It is Ego-less. But we must live within The Graph. We must remain constantly in awe of its great efficacy, its immense beauty. We must allow The Graph to complete us, to satisfy us. We must not try and build elsewhere. Because we are not architects. And the land is unsuitable. There will be insufficient drainage. Our tools will be faulty, our contractors unreliable. Why build a shack, a slum, when we have a perfectly good house right here? Not a house, no, a palace, a castle. What would be the use in that? Who might hope to benefit? It's simply Ego, Mira A. It's illogical. It's just perverse.'

'A slum.' I nod. I am building a slum. It *is* perverse.

'We cannot apply sensible standards to wild theorising, Mira A.' Kite is trenchant. 'First there is an itch, then there is a gap, and then, suddenly, a strange and dangerous movement takes place...completely irrational, completely pointless, utterly destructive, utterly wrong.'
So many hard words! Like little rocks. Bouncing, bruising, smacking, grazing.

His eyes gaze at me most intently. 'We might call this movement A Leap of Faith...' he whispers.
I am startled by this notion. I am horrified.
An itch?

A gap?

A congregation?

A narrative?

A Cathedral?

A Leap of ... of *Faith*?

And then?

Then?

Then what?

Who?

'*HOW CAN I STOP THIS?!?*' I groan, clawing at my chest (although the fabric prohibits me).

Because suddenly I can't *breathe*! I can't *breathe* without The Graph! Not here! Not out here! In this awful, pointless, hollow realm. This haunted, broken, shapeless place. This lonely hinterland.

Is this The Past? Is this how The Past felt?

So light yet so airless? So numb and blank and cruel and meaningless?

With the itch? That dreadful itch, just gnawing and gnawing and gnawing and gnawing ... ?

'We will use chemicals,' Kite says, most determinedly, 'and we will adjust your Oracular Devices.'

I nod.

'You are not too far gone yet,' he says, patting my shoulder reassuringly. 'Perhaps focus on some new activities – acquire a pet. Take up another instrument. Have you considered the kora? I think it may suit you. Try to give more, to share more.'

'When will The Graph ... ?' I ask, glancing over nervously.

But Kite doesn't answer me at first. 'Remember that precious guitar?' he asks, with a slow smile. 'That precious guitar you found on the Stream with its strange, metal strings?'

The guitar? *Oh*. I start. I clench my hands. I quickly nod. I bite my lip.

'And you were perplexed by the puzzle?'

Yes. *Yes*. I nod.

'Well apparently there was no great mystery after all.' Kite chuckles. 'The guitarist was prone to sweating heavily – when he was nervous, during performances – and so his fingers would slip on the new gut strings. So he stuck to the old metal ones. He'd learned to play on metal. He persisted with metal. But the sound was too harsh and people hated it, they mocked and derided him. He became an embarrassment, a laughing-stock. So he added the dampers, to reduce the buzz. *That* was the puzzle. There *was* no puzzle. It was mere human fallibility. Sweat. Performance anxiety. Weakness. Imperfection. That was all.'

'The Graph...?' I repeat, hardly listening, my eyes bouncing from wall to ceiling to wall.

'Now!' he says, lifting both arms in a dramatic, swooping movement (as if girding an entire orchestra into a final crescendo), 'This Moment!' Then he bows sharply, deeply, and he leaves.

He's gone.

And it's back on! It's back on!
Oh thank…thank…

Who?

A gap.
A strange gap.
What was I thinking?

Who was I reaching for?

But The Graph!
The Graph!
It is back!

And at last.
At long last.
I can breathe.
I can breathe.
I can *breathe*.

6
The Kora.

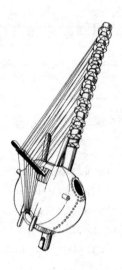

The kora originated in West Africa. It is a double-bridge-harp-lute with twenty-one strings. The strings descend in two, separate ranks and are played using the thumb and the index finger of both hands. The remaining fingers simply support the instrument. The tuning on the original kora was quite unstable and it was retuned by dint of leather tuning rings (or *konso*) which could be pushed up and down the neck providing four different seven-note scales. The Young, however, play a perfected version with tuning pegs.

There is something very calming about this ancient instrument. The notes hit the air like summer rain falling on fields of ripe wheat. So warm. So evocative. So joyful. So fresh.

Although replacing the old tuning mechanism with adjustable pegs means – my Sensor tells me – that the pitch is much more limited than on the original instrument, where the ability to modulate the subtleties of tuning was an intrinsic part of the skill of the player; a marker of experience, of knowledge, of excellence.

But The Young play a perfected instrument.

A limited instrument.

Modified.
Clean.
Curtailed.

I prefer the guitar.

While we're on the subject...
(*are* we on the subject?)
There is something about Ki...uh...about *you-know-who*'s
logo that worries me. The tail. The tail on the blue kite is now
slightly longer. There is an extra red ribbon at the end of the
tail, a new ribbon.

And it oscillates.

Am *I* the new ribbon?

Why did I have that thought?

I must stop telling the story.
I must stop building The Cath...
...the *you-know-what*.

The *you-know-what*.

Why is that italicised? Is it the way I'm thinking?

Might it be a clue?
A *clue*?

Perhaps?

Who am I telling the story to?
My sister star?
Who am I building the *you-know-what* for?

And why on earth would *you-know-who* tell me I was building a *you-know-what* in one breath and then call it a mere shack in the next?

That seems a little contradictory, don't you think?

There is no winter with the kora. It is always hopeful. Yet often wistful. And there is very little written history with this instrument. The tradition was passed down within tribes, within families, principally by mouth.

Perhaps that is why *you-know-who* was so keen for me to take it up. Because it is so old, but still new.

I wish I could stick with the kora. But the range is more limited. And my spare fingers grow tired of supporting the instrument. They tickle. They itch. They thirst for the tremolo. They thirst for inclusion.

No.

No more itching.

When I think back on the conversation with *you-know-who*, I start to...
There are many questions which I need to push away. Just turn away from.

Like:

Is the *you-know-what* a clue?

And why did he (*you-know-who*) mention the perspiration issue? Superficially to deflate me (to answer the puzzle that was no puzzle)...? Yes, superficially...but in fact he has only succeeded in piquing my interest. He has captured my imagination. He has inspired feelings not of derision or contempt, but of sympathy. And – worst of all – he has created a fresh neural pathway. Which was dangerous. Even foolish. He took a gamble. And the gamble, it seems, has lost.

Why did he do that?
Is it a test?
Is it a problem?
Is it a flaw in The System?
Is *you-know-who* mad?
Who *is* he?
Of course I could find out if I really wanted to. I could go to his Graph. In a mere instant. I could read his Information Stream. I am at liberty to do that. I am free to do that.
But I lack the confidence.
And I don't want to attract attention to myself.
Because I have been very good of late.
I have stopped talking to my sister star.
(Isn't that the phrase *you-know-who* used? Sister star?)
I have been playing the kora. I have joined a Kora Group. I have made several new friends who play the kora too. They have welcomed my sudden interest in their instrument.

There is Powys and Kipp and Tuesday and Cecil.

I asked Tuesday if she ever felt like the perfected version of the kora had limited the original instrument's natural range and delicacy. She looked confused for a moment, frowned slightly, slowly shook her head and then pushed the thought away. I saw her do so on her Stream. She just pushed the thought gently away. It was beautiful.

It really was quite beautiful.

Kipp patted me on the shoulder. 'The tuning is in our hearts, Mira A,' he explained, smiling, 'Perfection is not about the instrument itself – its leather rings or its pegs – but how we, The Young, choose to respond to the instrument. The tuning fork is in our hearts. Perfection is contained within us. It is something we express, something we cleave to. Even the most flawed object is perfect to innocent eyes. Eyes without prejudice. Eyes without haughtiness or need or expectation.'

Kipp has a way of expressing himself that I find utterly compelling and admirable. Kipp is very wise.

Of course I know all these things. I know all these things. But sometimes I forget them.

It's good to be reminded.

It's good to be reminded of how beautiful The System is. How clean. How innocent. How faultless.

The tuning fork is in our hearts.

I may stick with the kora after all. Because there is something missing. And when something is missing you have to
make up the difference yourself. You have to give more. Be
generous. Operate cheerfully within your limitations. Then
the limitations miraculously disappear. Or they cease to be
of concern. And that is good. That is the hallmark of The
Young. That is what we do because...

The tuning fork is in our hearts.

Is it just me, or is The Graph responding to verbal cues with
rather less precision of late? Less accuracy? Less dynamism?
The word 'miraculous' just slipped out, and my eyes darted
towards The Graph but there was no reaction.

This has unsettled me a little.
For a word like miraculous...
Oh. There you go.

It's as if...
As if...
I don't know.

I should just push this thought away.

The tuning fork is in our hearts.

I should strive to follow Tuesday's beautiful example.
I should strive...
Strive...

Strive...
Strive...
Strive...

That's better.

I should strive, but not too hard.
Never too hard.

7
The Bag of Stones.

The lucid dreaming and being Blinded By The Light: they continue, unabated, even after a recent, very minor adjustment of my Oracular Devices.
I gaze straight into the light as I say this...

The light *burns*...

Because – with hindsight – it occurs to me that *you-know-who* seemed to have no inkling about the dreaming and the Light.

Unless he did know – he *does* know – and this is simply a test.

I can't be sure.

But I am doing my best to adhere to the tenets of The System.

And look: I am happy. I am *happy*.

Happy.

No strange capitals!
No brackets!
No oscillating!

It must be the chemicals.

I have acquired a Neuro-Mechanical canine and I am exercising it very diligently. The Young may choose any breed of Neuro-Mechanical canine they like (small or large), but generally we choose a brown dog of medium build with a wagging tail and a mid-length nose and coat. A Labrador.

My Labrador is called Tuck. Tuck has his own very specific characteristics. He likes to be scratched behind his ears but growls if you try and touch his throat. To own Tuck I am obliged to relinquish certain other privileges. But I contribute to the net benefit of my Community (the Community of Energy) by spending set periods of time each day on my Power Spot.

And I exercise Tuck regularly. Tuck is energy-efficient, but I must work to make sure that he does not cause a depletion of energy on The Graph. Tuck has his own Graph.

Perhaps the leak has been resolved?

The oscillation is reduced.

I am happy.

Happy.

But still...

Because *you-know-who* mentioned (1) the precious guitar and (2) the heavy sweating and (3) the *you-know-what*, they have somehow entered my lucid dreaming. He forged a neural pathway.

Was it just an accident?

The first dream involved a bag of stones. I knew that I was dreaming. I glanced over at The Graph in my dream and The Graph was stable. I glanced into The Sensor and it was ticking. It was open. It was waiting.

I stared at the bag of stones and tipped my head the way I see Tuck tip his head when he is inquisitive. But I didn't ask a question to stop any trace of it being preserved on The Information Stream. The Sensor told me that there were a hundred stones in the bag.

But what did the stones mean? These hundred stones?

Then, as I quietly watched, a strong, male hand reached towards the bag and tipped the stones out on to the floor. It was an old floor of worn parquet.

Would The Sensor follow this hand? I did not ask. I just pricked my ear slightly the way Tuck pricks his ear. There was no actual movement, no actual pricking, just a tiny pulse, a minute intention.

The Sensor followed the hand.

I lay very still.

I am dreaming.

I mustn't wake up. I must follow the dream.

Oh...look. We are in a cheap boarding room of The Past. There is morning light. True light. How wonderful! And a man. He is seated in an old chair by an unmade bed wearing a clean vest, some pyjama bottoms and a small pair of glasses. He is holding a guitar. I shall not get too excited about this guitar. I will not let my heart race. But, yes, yes, it is the precious guitar.

It is the precious guitar!

I do not turn my head, I regulate my breathing, but I can also see, strewn over the rumpled coverlet of the bed, a collection of handbills and a newspaper. The Sensor tells me that we are in São Paulo, Brasil. The writing on the newspaper is in Spanish. On the handbill is a portrait of the man with the guitar, but he is in some kind of outlandish costume. He is bare-chested and wearing a feather headdress. He is daubed in paint.

There is a sudden, clattering sound and I am startled. I briefly hold my breath. I mustn't wake up.

Keep breathing Mira A! Keep breathing slowly and steadily!

The bag of stones has been emptied out on to the tiles. And then the man leans back in his chair, lifts his foot on to a small footstool and commences to play.

I wake up.

I am sitting bolt upright in bed.

Tuck is licking my foot! He has awoken me!

Aaargh!

Don't kick the dog, Mira A!
Push away that impulse. Yes. Just push it gently away...

I blink.

Agustín 'Chief Nitsuga Mangoré' Barrios.
That was the name on the handbill.
And he was playing *her* waltz.

And his lip – his upper lip – was covered in tiny stitches. All
along the top line of it. A neat train-track of stitches.

Why?

I pick up my guitar. I know that it is wrong to copy unfiltered
sounds from The Past because they are embedded with the
fallacies of History. The Young should play only the bones of
tunes – the skeletons – picked clean of myth and sentimen-
tality; we should only apprehend the plain shapes and then
improvise freely around them. Oh, but I cannot resist the
temptation to recreate the song – The New Song – which I
have only met in shadows, hitherto. Now I see its sweet face.
It is so peaceful and quiet, yet there is a hint of a wry smile,
a dusting of melancholy. But something even beyond that,

hidden behind the formal steps of the dance, the waltz –
what is it?

Of course I know that what I have dreamed is not real. This
wasn't secret footage of the guitarist from his private rooms
circa 1928. No. This is a curious splicing, an amalgam of
ideas, photographs, written text, recordings, objects and
hearsay forged into a four-dimensional document. And,
as such, it is dangerous. It is unreliable. How much of this
information is real? How much is simply my...

desire

(I stared into the light as I whispered that.)

My *desire* to hear that girl's tune.

(And again)

I start to play it. The first few notes I remember, and as I do so,
The Sensor prints up five words: *El Sueño de la Muñequita*,
then instantly translates: The Sleep of the Little Doll.
The original score, neatly handwritten, in all its inky imper-
fection, swiftly follows.
I don't ask anything.

I will not ask any questions. No. I will not make any assump-
tions. I cannot help this. Can I? No. *No.* I am helpless. I did
not create this neural pathway. *You-know-who* did that.

Those first few notes ...
Ah!
What joy!

I have found her.
I just keep on playing, and with every note she is more
intensely revealed to me.
And as I keep playing, The Sensor shows a pair of newly polished men's shoes, creaking.
It shows some floorboards. It shows a small girl (but not my
girl, this isn't *my* girl, she's younger, but she has the same
coffee-coloured skin and dark hair as my girl) and she is
glancing up at the elegantly turned-out stranger in the
shoes, frowning, and she is standing next to a cradle. And in
the cradle is a doll. The child places her finger over her lips.

Sssshhhhhh!

Ah. The doll is sleeping, and the elegant gentleman visitor
may inadvertently threaten to awaken her with the madden-
ing squeak of his new leather footwear!
So the man – I think we can identify this man, I think we
know his name – swiftly apologises and then produces his
guitar and makes up for this incredible faux pas with a little
waltz, a lullaby, to send the doll back to sleep again.

The man looks different, though. His face is notably changed
from how it first appeared in the dream.

Two words flash up on The Sensor:

TERRIBLE DISCIPLINE

Again, the bag of a hundred stones.

Each image partially covers the one that precedes it, but all move in a delirious conjunction, and as the eye glances back and forth between them, they happily nudge their way forward, springing back, once again, into sharper focus.

Following straight on from the stones – but with the stones – I am suddenly party to a snatch of conversation between… yes…the distinguished Uruguayan businessman, *aficionado* of the guitar and generous patron of the arts Martín Borda y Pagola and one of his workers…
    'Ah Señor, as a lover of music you must at all costs avoid the bowling alley near Melo. There is an ugly Indian there whose playing of the guitar is frightening.'

I hold my breath for a moment and halt my playing, fearing an EOE…

The moment passes and is followed by:

Sound of laughter.
Noise of a bowling alley.
A waft of guitar music.
Introductions are made.
Arrangements are forged.

Money is provided.

'But who would have thought it?' Borda y Pagola exclaims. 'That ugly young man plays like an angel!'

Sound of applause.

Ugly.

Frightening.

Indian.

More pathways are forged, are forging...

Next, a newspaper article:

'Mangoré presents himself with feathers. An anachronism. Something for children. His costume goes with the bamboo, but not with the guitar.

The reception by the public is cold and silent, with ironic comments: "horrendous", "shocking", "he's on marijuana" etc...'

Again, I hold my breath, I turn away...
But then, after a few moments:

'The Indian sits, strokes his instrument in a strangely smooth manner and begins. The program does not seem to be in agreement with the situation – it indicates the Indian

feels he is a musician, and that he wants to give the best he can, but my God! That savage wants to play 8.3.1.2, 41.5.22.51.8.02.5.5.2, 02.81.1.62.51.31, 41.9.61.51.8.3 on the guitar! It seems a sacrilege. We expect a disaster, a fatal musical calamity...'

An alarm goes off. The Sensor is temporarily disabled. The Graph is purpled, is flashing. I see a series of people on my Information Stream – alerted to this situation, this sudden crisis on The Graph – tuning in to find out what on earth might have happened. There is a flurry of concern, an atmosphere of confusion. I am under close observation. I am in turmoil. What was I thinking? To have been so thoughtless, so inconsiderate, so... so careless!

Hush, Mira A!
Hush!
Stop thinking!
Don't make things worse!

Stare into the light!

No!
No!
Don't!

I have gone too far this time. I should have listened to... there are ways... I was **greedy**, I was foolish, and now...
I close my eyes and feel an unfamiliar warmth, a strange heat in my cheeks. An awful feeling, this feeling...

Shame.

The buzz continues. What has happened here (I can see them thinking)? What is wrong with Mira A? What has she done? A vote was taken about the canine, wasn't it? We accepted the canine (an indulgence by any stretch of the imagination!). We all made allowances with regard to its impact on The Energy Graph. But now this? A History violation? Extraordinary!

I see other Graphs purpling in an awful flood of emotion. I see other people's anger washing through The Stream. A dreadful bruise. And I am at the core of it. I am its origin, its heart, its locus. The purpling extends way further than I could ever have considered feasible. A little tsunami of disapproval, of disappointment. The weight of it is unendurable.

Oh what have I done?
What was I thinking?

My eyes are now open and glued to The Graph again – The Stream – unblinking. But after merely a few seconds – thirty, at best – the purpling diminishes. The Young are pushing away their anger, their irritation. They are turning away from it. And I must do the same, although it feels like a struggle I am barely equal to.

Push it, Mira A. Push it away.
You must not live in regret.
Play your part, Mira A.

Deep breath.
Deep breath.
Push it away.
Push it away.

I place down my guitar. I try to compose my features.

All shall be well.

The tuning fork is in your heart.

All shall be well.

I hold out my hand to the dog, to Tuck, but he just sits and he gazes at me, his head hung down, his tail horribly still, his loyal brown eyes full of a deep and abiding disappointment.

8

The Forked Tongue.

After the EOE I thought *you-know-who* might pay me another visit.
I was dreading it.
But he didn't. He hasn't.
Although he appeared to me in a dream.
It was very vivid.

And even in my dreams he seems to generate nothing but trouble and anxiety.

Generate?

?

I have been playing the kora. I have been focusing on the kora. And I have been walking the dog. I have even been running on my Power Spot. If I run on my Power Spot twice a day I can counteract the energy consumed by my Neuro-Mechanical canine by generating energy of my own which is of a significantly higher range on The Graph.

It is exhausting.
I am tired.
But I am not resentful.
I am H(A)PPY.

Oh. Yes. I probably forgot to mention – it's back.
The disambiguation. The oscillation.

As I run on the Power Spot I try not to think about how people – other people on The Stream, The Young – conceived
the dog as an indulgence. Was Tuck not the idea of *you-
know-who*, after all? I had no thought of getting a pet before
you-know-who suggested that I should.

I was perfectly H(A)PPY with my guitar.

At least I think I was.
Before the photo of the little girl with the sad eyes and The
New Song.
Was that really the start of everything? Or was there some-
thing before? Something so subtle and faint I can hardly
remember it?

Why did I refer to her eyes? Her sad eyes?
Is that how I think of her now?
Are her eyes sad?

And I must avoid that word.
Pet.

It has certain connotations. The Graph doesn't like it.
I must be more careful.
Yes.
More aware. More tentative.

I accept this thought and then I gently push it away again.
I push it away.
I shouldn't worry.
I should just push it away.
And start over.

I am tired.

So much pushing.
Of so much pushing away.

I push this thought away.

Since my EOE and my...

TERRIBLE DISCIPLINE

Oh!
There it goes...

I don't know why this phrase keeps flashing up at random
on my Stream when I have not consciously thought it. And
the little asterisks. I don't understand those, either. Where
is this coming from? Is it a kink in The System?

It unnerves me. It could happen at any time and automatically place my Graph in jeopardy.

I have no control over...

TERRIBLE DISCIPLINE

It feels like a kind of madness.

And I need to counter it – the possibility of it, the randomness of it, the unexplainedness of it – with endless bouts of uplifting positivity.

The tuning fork is in your heart.

Yes.

I have been being positive.

Very positive.

And I have not touched my guitar in ages. Not since the EOE. I *can't* touch it. When I touch it I feel a deep sense of...

Shame

I looked into the light as I thought that.

Because I can't admit to this unproductive emotion publicly. But that is how I now feel.

I can push it away, quite easily (the idea, the prospect of sh... *you know*, etc). But when I actually move towards the guitar – when I pick up the guitar – the feeling of *you know* engulfs me. It is completely overwhe... oh-oh...

Oh well.

You know.

The anxiety is ever-present. That I will do something wrong again. Or that I will be advised badly and then do something wrong because of the bad advice I have been given.

I had no idea that the canine would generate so much ill feeling. I wish I could get rid of Tuck. Just push him away, like a bad thought. But that would indicate a measure of inconsistency, a lack of due seriousness, an inability to...

TERRIBLE DISCIPLINE

... to commit. And these tendencies couldn't help but affect The Graph negatively.

I feel like I am such a disappointment to him. To Tuck. Although I am probably just projecting how I feel about myself on to Tuck. Tuck is only a Neuro-Mechanical, after all. He is not real. But I am projecting what I feel about myself on to him because I am disappointed in myself. And I am telling the story again (aren't I?) because I feel the need to unburden myself about the guilt I am carrying.

TERRIBLE DISCIPLINE

I have unwittingly become involved in something beyond my understanding.

The tuning fork is in your heart!

I have added an exclamation mark (*heart!*) to denote how emphatically I am feeling this...But I need to be extra careful, just in case my repeated use of the phrase becomes slightly hysterical.

Sorry.

What kind of a narrative is this?
Is it a Mystery?
A Tragedy?
A *Whodunnit*?
Oh, if I could only make sense of it then perhaps I might be able to break the cycle, to tighten my resolve and stop constantly harking back.
I have tried to be silent.
I have tried to stop talking.
I have pushed and pushed. I have turned and turned.

TERRIBLE DISCIPLINE

But without the guitar I am lost.
My attachment was stronger than I could ever have thought possible.
You-know-who was right about that.
It is wrong to feel so attached. It is **dangerous**. It is weakness. It is betrayal.
So I am turning away from it.

But my fingers itch and rub aimlessly against each other. My mind *pings* and then loses all tension, like a broken string. And I am rehearsing The New Song as I sleep.

I can't help it.

It is my release.

When I stopped rehearsing it (because of *you-know-who*), I had nothing to occupy myself with as I slept. I was fighting all the time not to let...*you-know-what* echo within me – this massive structure whose door, it seems, is constantly open. Sometimes I peek through the door (this giant, ancient, oak door) and I peer into the gloom. There are others with me, outside, peering in. Who are they? What are they looking for? I can hear someone practising the organ. I think I recognise the piece. Something reminiscent of the works of 8.3.1.2. Stately. Full of broad, horizontal chords. And there is a person crouched in one of the pews...

Is it a man?

Or might it be a woman?

They seem to...somehow...oscillate.

But then I turn away. I push the thought away. Even as I sleep. I resist. I resist! Because I know that I am being drawn into something bad – or something forbidden, at the very least. And I need to pull this building down. I promised *you-know-who* that I would. I promised faithfully. And I try to stand by my promises. But still, *still*, I wish that he had never created the neural pathway to this place. It is embedded into my unconscious mind so deeply. Plumbed into the dark recesses.

Of course there are always the standard dreams that The Sensor provides. These are to keep The Young's guard up and to build our morale. And my sleeping self dutifully watches these dreams, but with one eye only... The other eye is scanning the horizon, looking for clues. My sleeping self feels an indefinable gap... a distance.

'Are these *my* dreams?' the sleeping Mira A asks. Sometimes she shouts, '*Whose dreams are these?!*' and bursts into noisy tears.
The Young never cry. Never. Because there is no need. Why would we? Why should we cry? It is so messy and self-defeating and so... so *damp*.
On one occasion...

TERRIBLE DISCIPLINE

On one occasion *you-know-who* appeared in my dream and began whispering things into my ear.

I could use his name freely because I was asleep and different rules apply there. I *knew* I was asleep. I was startled by his impertinence. I said, 'Why are you in my dreams, ****? What is the meaning of this?'

He responded with a question of his own: 'Why aren't you watching the standard dreams, Mira A? They're generally very good for morale building. Don't you think they might prove helpful?'
As he spoke I noticed that all his teeth were black.

'I am trying, ****,' I said, somewhat unnerved, 'but I feel a distance. I feel a gap between myself and these dreams.

And I don't know what to do with it – this gap. I don't know how to fill it.'

'Have you been...

TERRIBLE DISCIPLINE

'...playing the kora as I suggested?' **** asked.

'Yes,' I nodded. 'Although I find the perfected tuning to be a little unimaginative. The range of...'

'*The tuning fork is in your heart,*' **** avowed, then licked his lips. His tongue was forked.

'I know.' I shuddered, slightly unnerved (not so much by the tongue – I knew I was dreaming and that my feelings towards **** were mixed, at best – but by the idea that **** had been following my Information Stream. And if this was so, then why had I not been informed by my Sensor about it?). 'Uh...but it's interesting to note that as the instrument was originally conceived...' I waffled (of course this was a dream, a dream, that's why, just a dream...).

'Our kora is perfected,' **** interrupted, with a shrug.

'I know. I understand that. But this is an ancient instrument and the value of its—'

'Do you think you – *you* – Mira A, know better than The System?!' **** asked, indignant. His tongue flickered between his lips.

'Of course not!' I was naturally horrified by this idea. 'But the secret of the instrument...'

'Secret?' **** echoed, warily.

TERRIBLE DISCIPLINE

'To hold the tune is part of the skill of playing. It isn't something that can simply be ... '

Suddenly, I was showing **** what I meant. I went to fetch my kora. I removed it from its case. I unfastened the strings from the tuning pegs. I extracted the tuning pegs. I printed up some leather cords and carefully bound the strings with them at fixed intervals around the neck.

It took me several hours. All the while **** watched. He was very engaged. He was interested. He did not attempt to interfere or to interrupt. In fact it would be no exaggeration to confess that he may almost have ... have *inspired* me in my undertakings by his quiet, reptilian presence.

After the cords were attached, I used The Information Stream and The Sensor to guide me with the new tunings. But for some, strange reason the sound processing jarred me. It simply didn't feel right. It felt all wrong. So I took the liberty of manufacturing a special aluminium tuning fork in the chord of A (440Hz) – I took this liberty because I was dreaming, of course. It was a laborious process, all told. But **** watched, patiently.

It felt as if days had passed, weeks, even, until eventually the instrument was prepared. At last, at long last, I began to play. No. It was off. I scowled. I retuned. I played again. No. Still off. I retuned. No. No. *No. No.* It was immensely challenging. I was exhausted. I was spent. I was drained. I was dripping with perspiration ...

TERRIBLE DISCIPLINE

...but so...so...*engaged*, so *fulfilled*.

TERRIBLE DISCIPLINE

...and I was finally – ah, finally – about to get some kind of handle on the whole, complex tuning issue (although something still nagged and jarred in my ear) when * * * * stood up and left. Without a word. On the chair where he had been sitting was the transparent skin he had shed. It rustled when I touched it like the skein of a dried leaf.

Am I still dreaming? I wondered.
I looked around for Tuck. Tuck was nowhere to be seen. And the walls of my room were hung with a selection of animal corpses. From very small to very large. I saw a fieldmouse, strung up by its tiny ankles, and at the furthest extreme...

TERRIBLE DISCIPLINE

...I saw a giant black rhino.

All dead. All utterly dead. But peaceful. I was still dreaming. I felt tired. I put the kora back into its case and lay down on my bed. I fell asleep.

In the morning I went for a lengthy run on the Power Spot. I took Tuck for a walk. Tuck longs for me to throw him a frisbee – the way we used to play before the EOE – but I have stopped using the frisbee now because I worry about Tuck's excessive energy usage. But still Tuck asks for the frisbee and leaps around wildly in frustration when I do not offer it. It's immensely irritating. To see him consuming energy to no particular purpose. I wish I had never committed to this pet. Perhaps I can get him retuned. Tuck is a burden. Tuck really is a serious pain in the neck.

I push this thought away.

After I had exercised Tuck I attended a seminar about symmetry. It was fascinating – especially from the standpoint of musical composition. After that I made my weekly sojourn to volunteer in the soil laboratory. The work The Young are doing there is truly inspirational. We have come so far. I am awed by our dynamism, our meticulousness, our care.

A second run on the Power Spot was followed by a meeting with my Kora Group. For the past few sessions...

TERRIBLE DISCIPLINE

...we have been working on a piece based on the bones of a collaboration between a kora player and a harpist: 8.3.41.9.6–41.9.81.02.1.3 and 1.02.9.5.11–12.51.11.3.5.91. It's very beautiful. Tuesday plays the perfected harp quite wonderfully and so contributes 8.3.41.9.6–41.9.81.02.1.3's parts.

It had been a positive day thus far, and my Graph – my Information Stream, my Sensor – had given me no reason to believe that anything untoward had occurred or was about to occur. There were no signs, no clues, no vague indications that everything was about to go so terribly wrong. None.

When I entered the meeting room (slightly late after my exhausting exercise session) the other group members were clustered together, their individual Sensors interconnecting to form a large, communal screen. I idly imagined that they might be watching our joint performance from a previous session to gauge how well the collaboration was progressing. But I was way off the mark. They were actually...

TERRIBLE DISCIPLINE

... poring over the consolidated footage of intimate details of my day. Yes. They were watching *me*. They were studying *me*. Mira A. The large screen was divided into several parts. In one part I was running on the Power Spot and I was plainly exhausted. My Graph was pinkening quite dramatically because of the excessive and – quite frankly – unnatural levels of effort I was expending. I shuddered at the sight of it. My behaviour was silly. It was inappropriate. It was utterly counterproductive.

(How had I not realised? How had this plain truth escaped me? This activity was bogus and completely self-defeating!)

On another screen I was playing with Tuck, but Tuck was pestering me for the frisbee, and I was gradually losing my temper with him. At one point I actually – I hate to admit this, even to myself – yelled inarticulately and lashed out at him with my arm. I slapped him away! And The Graph, quite naturally, purpled significantly. The assembled party – watching, in shocked silence as this awful scene unfolded – all gasped, in unison.

Perhaps I have grown so accustomed – so hardened – to my Graph pinkening (and even purpling) of late that I have actually forgotten how shocking it really is, how dreadful it might appear – to Clean, Young eyes, to Neuro-Typical eyes – how strange and A-Typical and unsettling.

But these were just the small parts – the small parts of the big screen. The main part was taken up with footage of me that had been recorded the previous night. It was dark. But I was hard at work re-stringing and retuning my kora.

The tuning fork is in your heart!

TERRIBLE DISCIPLINE

And all the while as I retuned it my lips were moving. I was talking to myself. No, *no*, I was talking to Ki...to *you-know-who*, sitting on a chair close by. But *you-know-who* was not on the chair. Tuck was on the chair. Tuck was sitting, bolt upright, on the chair. I was talking to Tuck.

Someone in the group raised the volume on this odd-seeming monologue for a moment and my voice was suddenly audible. I was saying, 'The skill is embedded in the...the proficiency of...in the act of...the attempt to...to control the variable...which refuses to be controlled...which is imperfect...and this imperfection becomes...it's an essential part of the idea, ****,...the core of the idea...something so ancient and so imprecise...so capricious, so wayward, so erratic, so volatile, so mercurial...and this is the...this is the...this is the key, ****,...the heart...the source...this is the clue,****, the meaning is contained in the...the gap...the space...the void...'

And on the other screens, my voice, still exclaiming, 'I must keep going. Just a minute longer. I must, I *must*...

Oh, but I'm so tired, so tired, so tired, so *tired*...'
and:

'Down, dog! Down! *Down!* Stop it! *Stop!* This is *awful!*
Down! *Down!* I *hate* you! I *hate* you! You're completely
unbearable!'

I had never realised before how irritating the grain of
my voice is. So puny. So nasal. So whiney. So...so...*bleating*, so insubstantial, so partial, so unappealing, so...so
unfinished.

Kipp scratched his head and then muttered to the assembled group: 'Please note: there's no evidence of purpling in
the coverage on the big screen...'

'She's asleep,' Tuesday muttered, apparently astonished.

'This isn't me,' I blurted out.

They all turned, *en masse*. The look in their eyes – surprise,
judgement – was excruciating. I dropped my kora case and
covered my face with my hands. Kipp – who is so pure, so
rational, so inspirational in his detachment – was instantly
by my side. 'I'm sorry, Mira A,' he murmured, 'we did not
mean to spy on you. We admire you. We trust you. We value
your contribution to the Kora Group. But you were late and
someone happened to glance at your Stream to find out...
and then...because of the...I suppose...the recent EOE,
your Stream was suddenly very bumpy...it kept...there
was a vibration...an...an oscillation...and everything
began playing, all at once...so we were concerned...sur-
prised...and gradually our Sensors became unified until
we were all just...just standing here and...just...just
watching.'

'But I can explain, I can explain...' I babbled.

'You are too upset,' Tuesday interrupted. 'Look…your Graph is purpling. We can't afford another EOE. We are in the Kora Group together. We can't allow the Kora Group to become implicated in this. The Kora Group is a very happy organisation, a very Fresh and Clean organisation…'

'Weren't we in that seminar about symmetry together,' Powys suddenly piped up, 'earlier today? And now, the Kora Group? If both of these Communities become implicated in your purpling it will critically affect the Balance in at least *two* of my activities. *Two* of my Graphs – my Communities – at the very least, will be implicated. So calm down. *Please* calm down. We are all turning away. Everything we have seen…Look' – he held out a hand towards the others, their Graphs – 'look…check our Graphs if you don't believe me…we are calmly turning away. All of us. It is forgotten. It is all forgotten. We have already moved on. We are here, in This Moment.'

'Mira A must try and control her emotions' – Kipp nodded – 'but we can't just turn away entirely, Powys, because this is serious. This is very serious. There is evidence of a…' – he drew a deep breath and glanced towards his own Graph – 'a dangerous confusion here. A problem. Something is wrong with Mira A. She has retuned her kora. She has brought imperfection to her instrument. She has violated the code of the kora.'

Tuesday shuddered as she watched Kipp's Information Stream lightly pinkening. It was too much for her to bear. Not just because she was concerned about Kipp (because Kipp had done nothing wrong, he was pinkening by implication) but because of what this pinkening might represent for herself – her own pristine Graph – and, more widely, the Kora Group's.

'But I was asleep, Kipp,' I croaked – I wheedled – my throat constricted with repressed emotion. 'I would never have...I would never have dreamed of—'

'But you *did* dream of...' Kipp interrupted. Then he regretted it. It smacked too much of criticism, of judgement.

'I apologise, Mira A. This is all rather confusing,' Kipp added.

'I don't know what to say,' Tuesday said.

As they were speaking I opened my kora case. Simply to prove them all wrong. I opened the case and I took out the kora. To show them. As evidence. But I was astonished to discover that it *had* been restrung! I *had* restrung the kora. This was *all real*. This was not some wild and unfathomable chimera. This was *all true*.

Then – quite unconnected to this fact – my heart almost stopped beating for a second, in pure fear, in horror, because I had mentioned *you-know-who*, by name (had I not?), openly, persistently, in my dream! There had been some pinkening. And now all these different Streams – the Streams of the Kora Group – were embedded with the idea of *you-know-who*. He was a part of my narrative. And the narrative had spread. And I could see, as I looked around me, in the faces of the Kora Group as they stared at the imperfect kora, the re-strung kora, that I had unleashed a question, a doubt, a bruise, among them. I had done that. I had done that. I had infected them. I had created a series of awful neural pathways.

Where might they lead?!

TERRIBLE DISCIPLINE

I had unintentionally (but *was* it unintentional?) spread corruption!
I had unwittingly (but *was* it unwitting?) declared war on The Young!
In my sleep!
Without even realising!

HOW?!
HOW COULD I MAKE THIS RIGHT?!
HOW?!

I quickly placed the kora back into its case.

'I will destroy this kora,' I said. 'There will be no trace remaining. It is an insult to the perfected instrument, a dreadful...a terrible violation. I'm so sorry, Tuesday,' I interrupted myself, 'but in order to describe what I have done, how I have...

SINNED

I gulped, confused, incapacitated, cornered. 'There is a problem with my Oracular Devices,' I panted. 'An...an...an oscillation. They have tried to correct it. But they failed. I am sorry. I am so sorry. I have understood what has been said. I have understood it perfectly. The tuning fork is in your heart. I know that. I trust that.

The tuning fork is in your heart.'

Silence.

I saw a series of individual Graphs struggling to push what had just happened away. Pushing *me* away. Turning away.

'I must go,' I muttered, 'I must leave the Kora Group. I apologise from the very bottom of my heart for the negative impact I have had on this Community. It is a wonderful Community, a good, a generous, a H(A)PPY...'
Everything wavered. I quickly closed my mouth.

'About ****,' Kipp said, after a brief pause, 'I think you should seriously consider re-evaluating that situation. It's not right, Mira A. It's...' He paused nervously before using the word, '...*unhealthy*.'

'****?' I froze, just for a second, and then I squawked, loudly – strangely, inarticulately – because it was the only thing I could come up with to stop everyone from glancing over towards my Stream (on which ****'s identifier, his distinctive logo, was currently flashing).

'Yes. I'm not sure if it's really working out between the two of you' (Kipp was clearly somewhat perturbed by the squawk). 'Perhaps consider exchanging him for a Neuro-Mechanical feline, or a bird. They might prove less of a psychological burden.'

I was silent for a second, not quite knowing how to respond, and then, 'Yes,' I murmured, 'you're right. I *am* struggling. Thank you.'
I left the Kora Group, shamed and defeated, *confused*, with the imperfected kora.

Nobody tried to stop me.

I did not correct him. I left him – Kipp, and the wider group, by extension – believing that *you-know-who* was...was simply the dog.

It wasn't a **lie**. No. *No.* Surely not? I just didn't correct...I didn't...I couldn't...because of the narrative...because of this **awful** narrative, this **toxic** narrative...which keeps on unfurling, which will not be quietened.

A lie.

A *lie*!

But only to...to *stop*...to *protect*...

Oh!

Cannot.

Must not.

Speak.

Think.

9
Tuesday.

I don't want to talk any more. I am done with talking. Yet still, *still*, something compels me to speak out. To tell.

I requested permission (as suggested per my Graph) to have my Oracular Devices readjusted once again. The surgical Neuro-Mechanicals worked on them at great length – with impressive diligence. I told the Team Head about the oscillation and the Devices have now been re-knitted with additional supports. It will take some time before my vision returns to normal. I must be patient. I *am* patient. There is a pressure in the head. It is inevitable. It is not pain. The Young do not feel pain. We are protected from pain. That is part of The System. That promise, that guarantee, is built into The System. No Pain. No more pain.

TERRIBLE DISCIPLINE

Sorry. Sometimes I think that. For some reason. I consciously think it. I interrupt my thoughts with it. It's just a hangover from the previous problem. It's become ingrained. But it will fade. If I am sensible and calm and turn away without any trace of rancour or resentment.

When I explain things I violate codes.
Not because I am evil. But because of the need to make things clear.
Transparent.
Honest.
The narrative is a sticky web. The more I squirm to get free, the tighter it envelops me.

Such a confusing tangle.

So...
No more explanations.
I must just...just *be*.
In This Moment.
I must find my clarity here.
In This Moment.

Although...
Although I am worried now that I have misrepresented the...how do I describe them without implicating them in my pinkenings? The...the TB.

Kora Group
(I stared into the light as I thought this. I have come up with two random and variable initials to protect them, to confuse the linguistic processing. Please forgive the tedious obfuscation).

And that is why I am narrating. Because I hate...no, *no*, too strong, Mira A, too harsh...because I don't like to think of an injustice being done them (how can I explain this idea – injustice – without using the particular word? Trying to curtail my...constantly attempting to...it's completely beyond my powers). Because when I described them previously (the MZ), it was quite coldly. It wasn't sympathetically. And – contrary to what may appear – I have not declared war on The Young. I would *never* declare...you know...on The Young. Because I love...I *support* and *admire* The Young. This idea of...of war did not exist in my mind until *you-know-who* placed it there. And the neural pathway was established.

Anyway. I turn away from this thought. Because I am of The Young. And I turn away, calmly, cheerfully. I am not full of resentment. I will not let things rankle and fester.

I am Young and I am happy with what and who and why I am.

I am complete.

I am Pure.

Yes.

And I have started up the narrative again only because I wish to defend The Young, and, more specifically, the...the CR. In case of further ramifications. I must establish a record. I must be meticulously fair.

After I walked away from the JA several things happened that I had not anticipated. Good things. Affirmative things. And I should have expected them to happen, because we are The Young and we are perfected. We are Clean and Pure.

There is no pain. No pain. But in moments of weakness there is sometimes the *idea* of pain. There is a suspicion of pain. But there is actually none.

What makes me doubt?

The clamps behind my eyes are larger and stronger now, but they will, inevitably, place a measure of pressure (as I slowly adapt, which I shall, I must) on to the casings of the brain. But there is not pain. Just a … a gap where I might imagine the pain would be if only I could feel it.

I must turn away from this thought.
No. *No.* Not 'must'. That is far too emphatic. I will turn away from this thought.

There. It is done.

I am Free.
I am Pure and Unencumbered.

And I wish I could escape this narrative, which seems determined to haunt me, but I cannot accept the idea of any form of injustice. There are too many loose strands. Because of *you-know-who* and the neural pathways he unwittingly established to the *you-know-what.*

I will not think about the door, and the figure standing near it.
Or the person kneeling in the pews.
Or the organ music.
Or the distant scent of frangipani flowers.

Frangipani flowers?

?

No. *No.* No more details, Mira A! Don't allow this strand to expand, to become ever more complicated, to divide and fork out and spread and … and pollute …

Frangipani?
Like sweet almond? Like marzipan?

I should just turn away from the narrative, shouldn't I? By re-engaging, by seeking to perfect something that is intrinsically flawed … Aren't I simply digging myself into a still deeper hole? Risking ever further damage?

But what about the stain? The bruise?

The lie in the Kora Group?

(I stared into the light as I thought that.)

How can I rectify the damage I have unleashed on The Information Stream? I can't. But I must. So I will simply outline what has happened, with regard to the PH, and I will not mention anything else. Although there *is* nothing else (truly) since my recent medical procedure means that I am being fed chemicals intensively which work to create interludes of deep blackness (to help my brain to fully adjust). This deep blackness is so deep and so black. I am gone from everywhere. There are no dreams.

Although before...

I can't mention it, but I must. But this is so strange and so unexpected that it can only be discussed while I am staring into bright light. I must prepare myself, because, following my surgery, to stare into light like this is exhausting and disorientating.

Here goes. I will keep it mercifully brief.
At least, I will try to.

In short:
I left the Kora Group and it seemed as if The Young (represented by individuals in the Group who are representative of all The Young – because we are One) had turned away from me. In horror. In disgust. I was an outcast – a pariah. That was how I felt. And I did not blame them. I felt this same disgust myself. I was ashamed.

But it was not true. They had not turned away. Because over the next day or so my Sensor brought me a series of warm messages from those individuals, who thought of me, very often, it turned out, with such fondness, such hope, such kindness and sincere concern.

It was beautiful. A great balm.

Like a soft shower of apple blossom.

In fact I had no inkling – *none* – before I betrayed The Young of how... how greatly *valued* I am by my various Communities. I had no inkling. Only now – in my violations of the code – have I been made aware of this new reality.

Is it a new reality?

And so a neural pathway has been established – which I have yet to figure out or to understand, or even to accept, entirely – about how my having done wrong has made me more... I should not use the word but I can, I must... *loved* by my peers.

Isn't that odd?

I felt like the very opposite must be the case.

But it seems as if the ability – the requirement – to forgive, renders The Young still more Perfect, still more Pure, still more strong and free and generous.

I can't entirely understand it.

I'm not sure if The System has provided for this tendency.
Although The System is Perfected.
I should not question The System.
I should never question The System.
No.
I won't.
I can't.

My eyes are burning.
It is not pain, but it is the idea of **pain**.
I have turned away from the light for a brief second...
Please bear with me.

TERRIBLE DISCIPLINE

Oh, there was such affection, such tenderness, such *Community* in the Group that I was startled. I was unsettled. I almost began to doubt the rights and wrongs of things.

I am staring into the light again.

It was around this time that I received my first visit from Tuesday. She arrived at my room unannounced. I was surprised to see her. Of all the members of the Kora Group I would presume to say that Tuesday is the most tentative, the most Clean, the most Pure, the most fearful. And yet here she was. With me. Mira A. Who had behaved so miserably and indiscreetly. She had brought me a special harness for Tuck which she'd printed using her own, small personal allotment of resources and energy slightly earlier that day. It could be strapped around his nose and would, she claimed, make him easier to control as we walked together. There was a special technique that needed to be employed. A sharp but not aggressive sideways movement. And it worked a treat on Tuck. In retrospect I can't help thinking it's possible that a positive reaction to this device has been pre-programmed into Tuck's behavioural map (to render him more real, more legitimate) and that another person will traditionally assist the new owner of a Neuro-Mechanical canine by gifting it to them. That would make sense. A Community of Canine Care. A new Community. A new Graph.

I forgot to ask Tuesday if she owned or had once owned a Neuro-Mechanical canine herself. It is sometimes difficult to talk with Tuesday in a relaxed and open manner because of her immense stillness, her carefulness. I am always very aware of the fact that if I inadvertently say something to pinken my Graph while we are conversing together, this will instantly reflect badly on her. The maintenance of a pristine Graph is, quite naturally, of immense importance to Tuesday.

We are very different.
But we are One.
We are The Young.

I know little about Tuesday in general, except that she plays the kora and the harp very well and that she has a lively interest in The Simulation of The Real. She is strongly committed to this valuable programme and its wider Community.

On my second meeting with Tuesday she asked if she might help me by exercising my Neuro-Mechanical canine in the aftermath of my Oral Adjustment.

TERRIBLE DISCIPLINE

Of course I had been very careful not to use Tuck's name in front of her (and perhaps this was also a reason for the lack of conversational flow – of strange unease, of tension – between us). I couldn't take the risk that she might remember the way Kipp had incorrectly used ****'s name on that previous occasion. I couldn't risk her becoming consciously aware of (and therefore implicated in) the lie of my omission. That she would judge me. Or that a neural pathway would form and corrupt her involuntarily.

It eventually transpired that I had been worrying over nothing. Because when Tuesday asked if she might exercise Tuck for me, she used his name: Tuck. Then she removed a tiny, organic solar-simulator and a pocket puzzle from her bag and suggested that we might sit at a table together to play with it, briefly. These puzzles are very popular among The Young because they train the brain to perform at even higher levels (although we take no pride in solving these puzzles and other, comparable achievements – why should we? – since all The Young have equivalently high IQ levels).

My heart was beating fast, but I did as she asked. She was very particular about how we should sit. She moved the chairs into a new position. Then, after we were seated, she positioned the organic solar-simulator as if to shed light on the puzzle (which was a non-integrated diamond-shaped puzzle based on partially configured algebraic formulations) and shone it directly into our eyes.

'You know about staring into the light,' she murmured. I didn't answer.

The tuning fork is in your heart!

'I saw his logo on your Stream,' she continued, all the while blindly moving around the puzzle on the table, her voice completely calm and even, 'when Kipp inadvertently used the name Kite at the Kora Group meeting. If Kite has visited you it means that the Design Team are watching. When they interfere with your Oracular Devices it's a sure sign. And the dog. The canine. They gave Powys a canine. It generated jealousy among his Communities. It made him very fearful of judgement.'

She paused for a second. 'Stop blinking,' she said.

I tried to stop blinking.

'Kite has a duty to eliminate all kinks in The System. His is a laudable and entirely necessary occupation. I would never suggest otherwise. Although it's distinctly possible that *he* developed the kink in you and then sent you along to the Kora Group as a stooge – perhaps with the intention of trying to reel in a bigger fish.'

'Stooge...?' I stuttered, confused.

TERRIBLE DISCIPLINE

'Say nothing,' Tuesday interrupted me. 'Time is short. It may interest you to know that – aside from the other day at the Kora Group – I have been unable to map your journey because the signals on your Stream are strangely incoherent – they bounce and vibrate at an immense speed. This is unusual – disconcerting. But the plain truth is that I don't honestly *care* to find out what your journey is. What business is it of mine, after all? And I have no desire to get caught up in your narrative. All narratives, to my mind, are inherently bad and dangerous and only ever really exist as vehicles for a confused and over-inflated Ego. I utterly refuse – on a matter of principle – to risk creating any new neural pathways in my mind. Because I am Pure. I celebrate simplicity. If anything, I am an advocate of *reducing* neural pathways. But even so, your "incoherence" may be of use to me – to us. And that is why I have come here today, uninvited, to offer you a way out of your confusion. To offer you a New Certainty. This path – a cure for all your ills – is called The Banal.'

'Sorry…the…?' I stuttered.

'The Banal. We are a movement among The Young. And we are very powerful.'

'The Banal,' I echoed, somewhat warily.

TERRIBLE DISCIPLINE

Was this a trap?

'Yes. The word is generally perceived as having somewhat negative connotations, but the followers of The Banal understand that when something is banal it has a special, quiet power. A deep power. A profound and deadening power. This is the power that we celebrate.'

'Are you at war with The Young?' I whispered.

THE TUNING FORK IS IN YOUR HEART!

'Don't be ridiculous!' Tuesday snapped. 'The System is perfect. We just aim to preserve it and to consolidate it. By celebrating The Banal we hope to make it even stronger and still more Pure. But this isn't something you need to worry yourself about, Mira A. I just wanted to let you know that there is a way out of your confusion. There is a path you can take. The Banal offers you a new direction and a new kind of freedom. The Banal is a warm blanket. An end to all questions and doubt...'

She paused, concentrating on the puzzle for a second, then lifted her eyes to the light again. 'I also think it only fair to warn you about Kite – as a concerned member of your Community. He may mean you ill. I think you probably suspect this already. It's possible that the Technicians have detected a flaw way back in your genetic make-up – something ancient and unresolved – and they're doubtful that they can fully control it. They will have been watching you for years, even decades, waiting for it to develop. It will be something tiny but irresistible. An oscillation. An urge. And if your behaviour remains erratic, if you persist with your narrative, if you don't fully conform, they will have no other choice than to release you into... into... well, *you* know.'

She turned from the light again and looked deep into my eyes. There was something so immense and so terrifying in her stare that I felt completely stilled by it. Silenced by it. Tuesday's dark gaze was an end to all questions.

Tuesday returned her haunting eyes to the light again. 'Embracing The Banal may be your only way out,' she continued. 'I will allow you access to our movement if you follow the clues. If you betray us, however, I will solidify the lie about **** on to The Information Stream. You will be ruined. You will be lost…' She paused, then shuddered. 'Of course it must go without saying that there is no pressure or obligation – none whatsoever – for you to follow The Banal. You are perfectly free. You are Pure. It is your choice entirely.'

Then, before I could gather my thoughts together and muster a suitable response, Tuesday had turned off the solar-simulator and slipped it into her pocket. I glanced down, blinking, at the puzzle on the table. It was completed. Often puzzles at this level of complexity took many days, even weeks, to resolve. Tuesday had completed hers, automatically, while talking, in a minute or two, at most.

She quickly took her leave of me, but in the brief interlude prior to her doing so, I received four, separate notifications on my Stream volunteering to help me with Tuck during my recovery from surgery.

I didn't know what to make of it.

Was it a message?
Was it a clue?
Was it a trap?

I am so happy that Tuesday cares so much about me that she has decided to try and include me in her movement. To save me. What have I done to render myself a desirable recruit, after all? I am flawed. My Stream is bumpy. I am worthless.

And the others? The other members of the Kora Group? Are they also included in this secret about The Banal? I have no way of knowing.

All I do know is that I failed and my failure has been embraced by others with an immense generosity. With ... with *love*.

I do not use that word lightly.

Even while staring into the light.

Oh, but *is* it love, though?

Isn't love always disinterested?
Is this love disinterested?

Didn't Tuesday say that I might prove 'of use' to her in some way?

'Of use?'

I wish I had never joined the Kora Group! I wish that I had never seen the photo of the girl or read the article about the precious guitar! I wish that Kite had never reached out to help me and opened the door of The Cathedral!

And inside The Cathedral...?
Inside The Cathedral...?
Who is that?
Who might that be?
Kneeling, semi-obscured, in the half-shadow?

Who are they waiting for?
What are they doing there?

10
The Unknown.

Because The Young are Perfect and The System is Perfect and everything is Known...

But how can Perfection be 'consolidated'?
Wasn't that the word she used?
How can Perfection be improved upon?
Wouldn't that be simply a contradiction in terms?

TERRIBLE DISCIPLINE

I have lost my asterisks. But I try not to think about this (even positively) because I don't want to give them the incentive to return.

I am keeping a sharp eye out for clues from Tuesday (I am staring into the light as I say this). But my dreams still remain dark. Although now, lost in the darkness, I can sometimes intuit that the blackness is not solid or airy, but wet. A giant, black pool. Occasionally a drop of water disturbs the blackness, and the blackness ripples. But there is no sound, only silence – as if I am staring into an infinitely deep, black well.

One time I thought I may've seen a glimpse of Tuesday, reflected in the water, beckoning to me.
Jump in, Mira A!
Follow!
Follow me!
But I couldn't be really certain. It may only have been a synapse re-firing. Or my Sensor reconfiguring.

There is no need to worry. Because we are The Young.

And everything is Perfect and everything is Known.

Even The Unknown.
Even that.

The Unknown. The unmentionable. The unspoken contents of Tuesday's straight look.
The Unknown.
A tiny, blanched corner of our dear Mother, Earth, where the Imperfect are still permitted to wander and war and squawk. That place of immense filth and degradation, inhabited by the sordid, deluded and diseased remnants of shattered mankind. Watched and guarded by our Neuro-Mechanicals. A smudge. A violence. A contradiction. A horror.

Something The Young never speak of.

It must not be spoken of. The Neuro-Mechanicals have everything under control.

Because we are The Young and we are Pure. So we could not destroy them. We could only stand back and allow them to destroy themselves. We must permit all sentient creatures their own humble freedoms. And this is theirs. To live in misery and squalor.

They would not send me there.
Would they? To fail and age and die?

Why did she create this neural pathway?
The System says that for Perfection to exist it must have its opposite.
It needs its opposite.
There can be no Balance without imbalance.

The tuning fork is in your heart!

I must turn away from these thoughts.
These sudden fears.
But what if...?

Might The Banal be a way to save me from this horror?

From this place of age and pain and death and filth and war and rage? This place of no-sense. This place of prejudice and tribe and warped ideology. This place of violated gender. Littered with false Gods. The home of the jealous lie. The home of delusion and stewing resentment. The home of greed and lust and hunger.

A place of furiously turning towards (never away). A place of hate.

This small corner of our dear Mother, Earth, given over to bile and envy and confusion. Perfectly free to destroy its own freedoms. Fighting for them. Killing for them. Dying for them.

Ravaged. Transitory.

I must not tell the story of The Unknown.

The Unknown tells its own story.

The Unknown is entirely constructed out of false narratives.

Layer upon layer upon layer of them.

A million contradictions.

Wounded. Raw. Hopeless.

Would The Mechanics – The Technicians – send me there?

Because of the oscillation?

Oh what is this flaw in me?

Am I not Perfect?

Is this all just a trick?

A lie?

Are The Banal my answer? Can they resurrect me? Save me from The Unknown?

Is this how the narrative ends? Lost in The Unknown? Is

this how the narrative expands and then poisons? From within? A small gap that becomes a slight oscillation, then a brief confusion, then a gradual infiltration? Then a lie?

Every word, another nail in my coffin. Every word, a small shove towards imperfection, towards The Unknown.

must. stop.

I must enter The Banal. Surely? To save myself?
Oh let my dreams return!
Let the darkness fade! So I may hunt for clues! A way out of all this dreadful indecision. This monstrous story. These toxic words and...and...and...

and by virtue of his creative wisdom, Our father created

the foundation of human speech, And caused it to

form part of his own godliness. Before the earth

existed, In the midst of primeval darkness,

Before there was knowledge of things,

He created the foundation of future

human speech, And the first true father Namandu

Caused it to form part of his own divinity.

Having conceived the origin of future human

speech, Out of the wisdom contained within his

own godliness, And by virtue of his creative

wisdom He conceived the foundation of love

of one's fellow men. Before the earth

existed, In the midst of primeval darkness,

Before there was knowledge of things,

And by virtue of his creative power

He conceived the foundation

of love of one's fellow men.

Having created the foundations

of human speech, Having created a

small portion of love Out of the wisdom

contained within his own

godliness And by

virtue of his creative

wisdom He created,

in his solitude, The

beginning of a sacred hymn,

Before the earth existed, In the

midst of primeval darkness, Before there was knowledge
of things He created, in his solitude, the beginning of a

116

sacred hymn... Having created, in his solitude the origin of human speech; Having created, in his solitude, a small portion of love, Having created, in his solitude, a short, sacred hymn, He pondered deeply... and words and...

What?!

There are gaps...spaces. I can feel them. Strange spaces pushing their way in between the language.

What?!

A space.
And another space.
Blackness and whiteness collapsing each into the other...

A knock!
She turns from the light, blinking.
Was that...?
She glances towards her Sensor. It reads:

'word' and 'soul' are synonymous in the Guaraní language.

Guaraní?

She blinks. She looks again. A second knock (or is it a third?). The Sensor vibrates slightly and then her Stream tells her that it is Kipp. It is Kipp come calling. To exercise Tuck. He offered. Even though he had strongly advised her to return the dog (did he not? And that was the source of the...that was the beginning of the...).

Because the new clamps will take a while to establish themselves comfortably in her head. To embed themselves into her skull. Of course this process can – in some circumstances – be instantaneous. But hers is a special case. So the technique has been gently modified.

They are going to great lengths to rectify this problem. Even the Neuro-Mechanicals are surprised by the extent of it.

She is an anomaly.

Something in her is resistant.
Something in her will not give.
Something in her...
Something in her...
Something in...
Something in *me*...
In *me*...
In *me*

Something in *me* will not give.
Something in *me* refuses to oblige.
And the narrative.
That too.
It persists.

I...I...I...I am happy to see Kipp. Kipp is wise and Pure and good. Kipp is admirably Non-Attached. He asks m...me about ****'s new harness. 'Tuesday made it for m...me,' I stutter, seeing ****'s name pinkening on my Stream, 'and...and his name is...is *Tuck*. The canine's name is Tuck.' Kipp frowns for a moment, then he shrugs. He turns away from the situation. I see it on his Stream. He glances towards his Graph, then mine, and detects a pinkening. He turns away from this, too. He does not question or fly into a panic or call up earlier information to try and validate himself (or invalidate me). He just turns away, as we are meant to do. Because he is Good and he is Humble and he is Modest.

He quietly places the harness down on the table – he rejects the harness – and instead calls Tuck to his side with a low whistle. Tuck trots over and sits compliantly at his feet, looking up at him, tail wagging. Tuck trusts Kipp utterly, implicitly. Then Kipp asks me – out of politeness – about my recent procedure. I am struggling to focus. I am afraid. Because everything is so precious and so precarious. There is not pain, no. Not pain. But there is the idea...the idea of...

'Mira A? Mira A?'

Kipp is proffering me a glass of water. I am slumped over in a chair. Kipp is kneeling down in front of me.

'Mira A? Hello? Mira A?'

'What happened?'

'You collapsed.'

'Is she all right?'

'Pardon?'

'Am I all right?'

'Of course.' Kipp nods. 'I checked the information on your Hard Drive. There was a risk of dizziness. After the procedure. That's why you are being told to rest.'

'Is that really the reason?' I wonder.

'Did I say that out loud?' I wonder.

'You did say that out loud,' Kipp confirms.

'I wanted to return the canine, Kipp.' I reach out for the glass of water, but my hand is shaking too much to hold it without the risk of spilling it, so Kipp gently places it down on the nearby table.

'I wanted to return it, Kipp,' I repeat, 'but The Young have been so good. The CT have been so kind with all their offers of help and support...'

'The...?' Kipp is scowling.

'And then you...'

I can't mention it. I can't mention the *you-know-what*, can I? Or how my mistake has been the source of such...such kindness from...from him, from so many of the others. Kipp says nothing. He seems concerned.

'I heard about your lecture,' I continue, somewhat haltingly, somewhat hopefully, 'your lecture on The Banal, and I was planning to attend because I thought it might be a...a...'

Clue?

I dare not say it.

I glance over at my Stream. And there it is. Betraying me. Gently purpling. But Kipp does not look at my Stream. Kipp looks directly at me.

'There is no need for you to attend the lecture,' he says. 'There is nothing in it to interest you, Mira A. Nothing at all.'

'Oh, but I think there will be . . . ' I insist.

'No. *No*. Trust me when I say that there is nothing – *nothing* – in my lecture to interest or concern you. My lecture will be very dull – almost bland. My lecture, like its subject, will be trite and meaningless. In fact you should avoid my lecture *at all costs*.'

I frown, slightly startled by his sudden emphasis. Kipp is not given to emphatic statements. Kipp is always measured, always calm.

'Do you hear me, Mira A?' he continues. 'You should avoid the lecture *at all costs*.'

'Perhaps we need to shed some more light on this,' I murmur, reaching for the window blind.

'No.' He shakes his head. 'It is bright enough in here already. Stay in This Moment, Mira A. Turn away from doubt.'

Then he pauses before adding, 'We must believe in The Young, Mira A, because The Young are Perfect. You cannot improve on Perfection. You must turn away from anything – or anyone – who encourages you to think otherwise. You have been experiencing some problems with your Oracular Devices, but soon that will be rectified. Then everything will return to normal again. Don't be impatient. Be Hopeful. And be Happy. Just be Happy. In This Moment.'

'Perhaps it is too late,' I whisper, wishing for the light, yearning for the light. For the chance to speak freely.

'Turn away,' Kipp persists, 'just turn away from the things you don't understand. Trust in The System. The Young can only remain perfect if we are completely trusting.'

'But what about all the' – I clear my throat nervously – 'the neural pathways which I...I cannot...?'

'You have an excellent battery of techniques, Mira A.' Kipp smiles. 'Remember? You have been taught them by The System. *Use* them. And if you feel especially challenged, then...' – he glances around the room – 'then play a tune on your guitar. Improvise. You are musical. Lose yourself in a melody. Follow that. Trust in that. Then the problematic Pathways will fade. And always remember: the tuning fork is in your heart. The Perfection of The Young is in *you* – only you. It cannot be found elsewhere.'

The tuning fork is in my heart!

My Stream echoes his words in desperate italics.

I want to believe...I do...I *do*...

And now, at last, Kipp is inspecting my Stream. 'Without the italics,' he says, chuckling wryly, 'and the exclamation mark. Because everything is easy. Everything is calm. There is no need to stress. There is no need to worry.'

After a thoughtful pause he adds, with a slight frown, 'There is still a tiny tremor, I see. But it is less. It is much better than before. The new clamps are definitely beginning to stabilise.'

I smile back at him, hopefully.

Kipp is such a good person. He is such a positive example. He is so generous and so kind. She must not demand anything more of him. No. She has been silly and greedy. She ... she ... *I* ... we have taken up way too much of his precious time already.

Oh ... Oh ... Oh ...! If only I could escape the narrative I might save myself! The narrative is ruining me! The narrative is consuming me! And what will remain thereafter? Just two new clamps and a small pile of tinder? And a slight oscillation? And a gap? A hole? An echo? A question?

I am staring into the light.

Because I need to think. I need to weigh things up. I need to find out more and then decide what to do, once and for all.

Tuesday says there is a problem in my essential composition – a kink. Tuesday says – and it is something I have long suspected – that I am not Perfect, that I am imperfection.

A flaw.
A mistake.

The tuning fork is in your heart.

It's in your heart!
Your *heart*!

But if I am not Perfect, then why would Tuesday invite me to join The Banal? Is The Banal full of imperfection? Because surely to embrace imperfection would be to declare war on The Young? To form an organisation that wants to improve on Perfection? There is something odd and strange and illogical about that. Unless, of course, The Banal can cure me, can iron out my kinks, can smother the narrative and make me Clean and Fresh and Pure again…

Because I am not Perfect.
And if I am not Perfect, then…
Then what else is imperfect?
Who else?

Am I the nexus?
The first standing domino at the head (or the back) of a giant legion of others? The wobbling, unsteady, tipping domino threatening to take down everything with it? The whole edifice?

If I am that domino…
If I am that domino then I will sacrifice myself for the others.

I will sacrifice myself for The Young.
In a heartbeat.
Because I believe in The Young!
I trust in The System!
I do! I must!

But Tuesday...
Tuesday suggested that **** may have used me – may have planted the kink into me – as a way of gaining access to The Banal.

Is **** the nexus?
Is he the flaw?
The rot?

And if this is so (if... if I am the plant, the dummy, and **** is the nexus), then why would Tuesday still embrace me and bring me closer into Her Orbit?
Surely she would feel obliged – compelled – to push me away?
Because I am flawed and she longs for Perfection.
But perfection never rejects.
Although it does turn away.
Doesn't it?
Doesn't it?

And Kipp? Kipp is delivering a lecture on The Banal. But he tells me not to attend. Yet Tuesday has instructed me to keep a look out for clues.

But Kipp is decent and honest. He would not look into the light. Perhaps Kipp is secretly at war with Tuesday because Tuesday is secretly at war with The Young?

And Kipp came to warn me. Because Kipp – not **** – is the person who is gaining access to Tuesday, but without creating any ripples, any fresh neural pathways. Smoothly and honestly and quietly. Legitimately. He is fighting a battle without casualties. Because of his lecture. Which gives him access to ideas that he opposes – and which he will discredit – without the threat of bruising and infiltration.

This is a strange narrative.
Kipp's is a strange narrative.

It makes my mind

I trust Kipp. But I trusted **** at first – and look where I ended up: in an EOE! In the Kora Group. With a Neuro-Mechanical canine I didn't even want who filled the others with envy.

Caught in a lie that may yet implicate Kipp... A lie spreading, every second, within this narrative, like a bruise.

I do not know what to do.
I can only spew out words and words and words and words.
And to fuel the words I crave still more information.
Clues.

I am hungry. I am ravening. How might this craving be satisfied?

Perhaps I should follow their Streams? I could hunt for the answers there. But it is risky. Because if I follow their Streams there is the possibility that my lie, my bruise, my narrative, my gap, my pinkening and purpling, will affect them inadvertently.

They will know that I am watching them. The Stream never lies. At least...

It will seem odd. It will seem...inappropriate. Intrusive.

But what other choice do I have?

The tuning fork is in your heart.

If only I could dream. I might follow them there...

Turn away, Mira A!

TERRIBLE DISCIPLINE

Perhaps the oscillation will protect me. Mask my interest. Be my armour.

Or perhaps...

What?

What?

What?!

The guitar?

11

The Gaps.

This awful feeling of shame when I approach the guitar. What is it? Guilt? *Sin?* This awful feeling of shame when I approach the guitar. What is it? Guilt? *Sin?* This awful feeling of shame when I approach the guitar. What is it? Guilt? *Sin?* This awful feeling of shame when I approach the guitar. What is it? Guilt? *Sin?* This awful feeling of shame when I approach the guitar. What is it? Guilt? *Sin?* This awful feeling of shame when I approach the guitar. What is it? Guilt? *Sin?* This awful feeling of shame when I approach the guitar. What is it? Guilt? *Sin?* This awful feeling of shame when I approach the guita. What is it? Guilt? *Sin?* Th awful feeling ame when I appro the guitar. What is it? G *Sin?* This awful ng of shame w I approach the guitar. it is it? Guilt? *Sin?* Th ful feelin shame when I approach e guitar. What is it? Guilt. Th ful feeling of shame when I approach the guitar. What is it *Sin?* This awful feeling of shame when I approach the guitar. What is it? Guilt? *Sin?* This awful feeling of shame when I approach the guitar. What is it? Guilt? *Sin?* This awful feeling of shame when I approach the guitar. What is it? Guilt? *Sin?* This awful feeling of shame when I approach the guitar. What is it? Guilt? *Sin?* This awful feeling of shame when I approach the guitar. What is it? Guilt? *Sin?* This awful feeling of shame when I approach the guitar. What is it? Guilt? *Sin?* This awful feeling of shame when I approach the guitar. What is it? Guilt? *Sin?*

The Graph is pinkening and purpling. I can't control it. Pinkening and purpling. The Graph is pinkening and purpling. I can't control it. Pinkening and purpling. The Graph is pinkening and purpling. I can't control it. Pinkening and purpling. The Graph is pinkening and purpling. I can't control it. Pinkening and purpling. The Graph is pinkening and purpling. I can't control it. Pinkening and purpling. The Graph is pinkening and purpling. I can't control it. Pinkening and purpling. The Graph is pinkening and purpling. I can't control it. Pinkening and purpling. The Graph is pinkening and purpling. I can't control it. Pinkening and purpling. The Graph is pinkening and purpling. I can't control it. Pinkening and purpling. The Graph is pinkening and purpling. I can't control it. Pinkening and purpling. The Graph is pinkening and purpling. I can't control it. Pinkening and purpling. The Graph is pinkening and purpling. I can't control it. Pinkening and purpling. The Graph is pinkening and purpling. I can't control it. Pinkening and purpling. The Graph is pinkening and purpling. I can't control it. Pinkening and purpling. The Graph is pinkening and purpling. I can't control it. Pinkening and purpling. The Graph is pinkening and purpling. I can't control it. Pinkening and purpling. The Graph is pinkening and purpling. I can't control it. Pinkening and purpling. The Graph is pinkening and purpling. I can't control it. Pinkening and purpling. The Graph is pinkening and purpling. I can't control it. Pinkening and purpling. The Graph is pinkening and purpling. I can't control it. Pinkening and purpling. The Graph is pinkening and purpling. I can't control it. Pinkening and purpling. The Graph is pinkening and purpling. I can't control it. Pinkening and purpling. The Graph is pinkening and purpling. I can't control it. Pinkening and purpling. The Graph is pinkening and purpling. I can't control it. Pinkening and purpling. The Graph is pinkening and purpling. I can't control it. Pinkening and purpling. The Graph is pinkening and purpling. I can't control it. Pinkening and purpling. The Graph is pinkening and purpling. I can't control it. Pinkening and purpling. The Graph is pinkening and purpling. I can't control it. Pinkening and purpling. The Graph is pinkening and purpling. I can't control it. Pinkening

I must turn away from these thoughts. Just turn away from them. I must. I *must*. I must turn away from these thoughts. Just turn away from them. I must. I *must*. I must turn away from these thoughts. Just turn away from them. I must. I *must*. I must turn away from these thoughts. Just turn away from them. I must. I *must*. I must turn away from these thoughts. Just turn away from them. I must. I *must*. I must turn away from these thoughts. Just turn away from them. I must. I *must*. I must turn away from these thoughts. Just turn away from them. I must. I *must*. I must turn away from these thoughts. Just turn away from them. I must.

away from them. I must. I *must*
Just turn away from them. I
these thoughts. Just turn away
away from these thoughts. Just
I must turn away from these t
must. I *must*. I must turn awa
from them. I must. I *must*. I mu
turn away from them. I must.
thoughts. Just turn away from
from these thoughts. Just turn
turn away from these thought
I *must*. I must turn away from
them. I must. I *must*. I must tu
away from them. I must. I *must*.

hts. Just turn
ıst turn away from these thoughts.
. I *must*. I must turn away from
ı them. I must. I *must*. I must turn
ı away from them. I must. I *must*.
hts. Just turn away from them. I
m these thoughts. Just turn away
ırn away from these thoughts. Just
ust. I must turn away from these
ı. I must. I *must*. I must turn away
from them. I must. I *must*. I must
ıst turn away from them. I must.
se thoughts. Just turn away from
vay from these thoughts. Just turn
ıst turn away from these thoughts.

Just turn away from them. I must. I *must*. I must turn away from these thoughts. Just turn away from them. I must. I *must*. I must turn away from these thoughts. Just turn away from them. I must. I *must*. I must turn away from these thoughts. Just turn away from them. I must. I *must*. I must turn away from these thoughts. Just turn away from them. I must. I *must*. I must turn away from these thoughts. Just turn away from them. I must. I *must*. I must turn away from these thoughts. Just turn away from them. I must. I *must*. I must turn away from these thoughts. Just turn away from them. I must. I *must*. I must turn away

Is there still an oscillation? But if the flaw has been corrected, if…if…then why…? Is there still an oscillation? But if the flaw has been corrected, if…if…then why…? Is there still an oscillation? But if the flaw has been corrected, if…if…then why…? Is there still an oscillation? But if the flaw has been corrected, if…if…then why…? Is there still an oscillation? But if the flaw has been corrected, if…if…then why…? Is there still an oscillation? But if the flaw has been corrected, if…if…then why…? Is there still an oscillation? But if the flaw has been corrected, if…if…then why…? Is there still an oscillation? But if the flaw has been corrected, if…if…then why…? Is there still an oscillation? But if the flaw has been corrected, if…if…then why…? Is there still an oscillation? But if the flaw has been corrected, if…if…then why…? Is there still an oscillation? But if the flaw has been corrected, if…if…then why…? Is there still an oscillation? But if the flaw has been corrected, if…if…then why…? Is there still an oscillation? But if the flaw has been corrected, if…if…then why…? Is there still an oscillation? But if the flaw has been corrected, if…if…then why…? Is there still an oscillation? But if the flaw has been corrected, if…if…then why…? Is there still an oscillation? But if the flaw has been corrected, if…if…then why…? Is there still an oscillation? But if the flaw has been corrected, if…if…then why…? Is there still an oscillation? But if the flaw has been corrected, if…if…then why…? Is there still an oscillation? But if the flaw has been corrected, if…if…then why…? Is there still an oscillation? But if the flaw has been corrected, if…if…then why…? Is there still an oscillation? But if the flaw has been corrected, if…if…then why…? Is there still an oscillation? But if the flaw has been corrected, if…if…then why…? Is there still an oscillation? But if the flaw has been corrected, if…if…then why…? Is there still an oscillation? But if the flaw has been corrected, if…if…then why…? Is there still an oscillation? But if the flaw has been corrected, if…if…then why…? Is there still an oscillation? But if the flaw has been corrected, if…if…then why…? Is there still an oscillation? But if the flaw has been corrected, if…if…then why…? Is there still an oscillation? But if the flaw has been corrected

This awful feeling of shame when I approach the guitar. What is it?
Guilt? *Sin?* This awful feeling of shame when I approach the guitar.
What is it? Guilt? *Sin?* This awful feeling of shame when I approach
the guitar. What is it? Guilt? *Sin?* This awful feeling of shame when
I approach the guitar. What is it? Guilt? *Sin?* This awful feeling of
shame when I approach the guitar. What is it? Guilt? *Sin?* This awful
feeling of shame when I approach the guitar. What is it? Guilt? *Sin?*
This awful feeling of shame when I approach the guitar. What is it?
Guilt? *Sin?* This awful feeling of shame when I approach the guitar.
What is it? Guilt? *Sin?* This awful feeling of shame when I approach
the guitar. What is it? Guilt? *Sin?* This awful feeling of shame when
I approach the guitar. What is it? *Sin?* This awful feeling of
shame when I approach the guitar. What? Guilt? *Sin?* This awful
feeling of shame when approach the guitar. What? Guilt? *Sin?*
This awful feeling of shame I approach guitar. What is it?
Guilt? *Sin?* This awful feeling of shame approach the guitar.
What is it? Guilt? This awful feeling of shame when I approach
the guitar. What it? Guilt? *Sin?* This awful feeling of shame when
I approach the guitar. What? Guilt? *Sin?* This awful feeling of
shame when I approach guitar. What is it? Guilt? *Sin?* This awful
feeling of shame when I approach the guitar. What is it? Guilt? *Sin?*
This awful feeling of shame when I approach the guitar. What is it?
Guilt? *Sin?* This awful feeling of shame when I approach the guitar.
What is it? Guilt? *Sin?* This awful feeling of shame when I approach
the guitar. What is it? Guilt? *Sin?* This awful feeling of shame when
I approach the guitar. What is it? Guilt? *Sin?* This awful feeling of
shame when I approach the guitar. What is it? Guilt? *Sin?* This awful
feeling of shame when I approach the guitar. What is it? Guilt? *Sin?*
This awful feeling of shame when I approach the guitar. What is it?
Guilt? *Sin?* This awful feeling of shame when I approach the guitar.
What is it? Guilt? *Sin?* This awful feeling of shame when I approach

I must turn away from these thoughts. Just turn away from them. I must. I *must*. I must turn away from these thoughts. Just turn away from them. I must. I *must*. I must turn away from these thoughts. Just turn away from them. I must. I *must*. I must turn away from these thoughts. Just turn away from them. I must. I *must*. I must turn away from these thoughts. Just turn away from them. I must. I *must*. I must turn away from these thoughts. Just turn away from them. I must. I *must*. I must turn away from these thoughts. Just turn away from them. I must. I *must*. I must turn away from these thoughts. Just turn away from them. I must. I *must*. I must turn away from these thoughts. Just turn away from them. I must. I *must*. I m turn away n these thoughts. Just turn away from them. I mus nust. I m arn away from these thoughts. Just turn away from em. I mu must. I must turn away from these thoughts. Just away fro em. I mu I *must*. I must turn away from these thoughts. Ju rn away n them. I must. I *must*. I must turn y from t thought st turn away from them. I must. I m must tu way from se thoughts. Just turn away from then nust. I m . I must t way from these thoughts. Just turn awa om the must. I m . I must turn away from these thoughts. Just turn a from the must. I *must*. I must turn away from these though ust turn y from them. I must. I *must*. I must turn away fro ese though. Just turn away from them. I must. I *must*. I mus urn away from these thoughts. Just turn away from them. I must. I *must*. I must turn away from these thoughts. Just turn away from them. I must. I *must*. I must turn away from these thoughts. Just turn away from them. I must. I *must*. I must turn away from these thoughts. Just turn away from them. I must. I *must*. I must turn away from these thoughts. Just turn away from them. I must. I *must*. I must turn away from these thoughts. Just turn away from them. I must. I *must*. I must turn away from these thoughts. Just turn away from them. I must. I *must*. I must turn away from these thoughts. Just turn away from them. I must. I *must*. I must turn away from these thoughts. Just turn away from them. I must. I *must*. I must turn away from these thoughts.

Can there be no end to these words and words and words and words and words? Can there be no end to these words and words and words and words and words? Can there be no end to these words and words and words and words and words? Can there be no end to these words and words and words and words and words? Can there be no end to these words and words and words and words and words? Can there be no end to these words and words and words and words and words? Can there be no end to these words and words and words and words and words? Can there be no end to these words and words and words and words and words? Can there be no end to these words and words and words and words and words? Can there be no end to these words and words and words and words and words? Can there be no end to these words and words and words and words and words? Can there be no end to these words and words and words and words and words? Can there be no end to these words and words and words and words and words? Can there be no end to these words and words and words and words and words? Can there be no end to these words and words and words and words and words? Can there be no end to these words and words and words and words and words? Can there be no end to these words and words and words and words and words? Can there be no end to these words and words and words and words and words? Can there be no end to these words and words and words and words and words? Can there be no end to these words and words and words and words and words? Can there be no end to these words and words and words and words and words? Can there be no end to these words and words and words and words and words? Can there be no end to these words and words and words and words and words? Can there be no end to these words and words and words and words and words? Can there be no end to these words and words and

Enough!

Enough!

ENOUGH!

Mira A inspects this word – *enough* – and is astonished by
its strangeness.
The curious sneeze of defiance that is *enough!*

She scratches her head, perplexed.
She glances around her.

Mira A picks up her guitar. She finds that she is perspiring
uncontrollably. Her hands are bathed in sweat. She tries to
play, to hold down a note – any note – but her fingers keep
slipping off the strings. She is disabled by an intense – a
burning – feeling of anxiety.

Turn away from the narrative!

Turn away, Mira A!

Mira A picks up her guitar. She is perspiring uncontrollably.
Her hands are bathed in sweat. She tries to play, to hold down
a note – any note – and her fingers, quite miraculously, seem
to adhere. But the note? Harsh! Metallic! Reverberating!
And the vibration enters her whole body through her fingertips – her skin – her pores – it echoes through her ears – it

shudders into her teeth.

This dreadful oscillation.
This flaw.
This blip.

But Mira A continues to strum, to pluck.

Be brave!

There is a tune she longs to play –

Be brave!

A sweet waltz. It is the only thing that may bring her solace.
She is not yet sure of it. She has not yet committed it to
memory. There are spaces. There are gaps. And sometimes
the gaps are more meaningful than the notes. She peers into
them. She marvels at their whiteness. She blinks. She looks
for her own shadow in the whiteness but there is no shadow
here.
There is nothing.

But narrative.

Must not panic.
Must not panic.

As long as she keeps telling the story.

She is alive.

She is not obliterated.

The words.

Her soul.

And yet…

But…

For some…

For some strange reason she suddenly can't…

Can't…

Uh!

Speak…

Can't…

Uh!

Can't…

Breathe!

Then the song returns. The darkness of the notes against the page. The waltz. Her fingers still perspiring. The curious oscillation.

Metal strings.

One hundred stones, rattling against the floorboards.

TERRIBLE DISCIPLINE!

One hundred stones.

And feathers.

And tiny stitches like a line of train track travelling across a broad upper lip.

She is dreaming, surely?

She is dreaming –

Yes! At last!

She mustn't wake up!

Don't wake up!

Sleep.

Sleeeeep.

Mira A sleeps, at first fitfully, then more deeply.

As Mira A sleeps, Mira B stares down quietly at Mira A's inert body, then glances over, faintly scowling, towards her Information Stream.

Mira B sighs and gently lifts her hand from where it has been firmly placed over Mira A's mouth. The marks of her fingers are clearly visible – indented, in angry pink, deep into Mira A's pale skin. After she carefully rearranges the dank locks of hair obscuring Mira A's damp cheeks she is still for a moment, then smiles darkly and bends forward, placing her lips right up close against Mira A's ear:

Hello. Hello. Hello. I am the sister star, she whispers.

12
The Light.

I am staring into the light.

I have started to tell the story of myself. As if I am distanced from myself – dispassionately watching myself. This narrative is the problem. It is a filth, a cancer, that infiltrates everything, that warps and undermines all that is sure and Known. All Certainty. All that is Present. All that is in This Moment. All confidence. All H(A)PPI...

There should have been a sense of relief at my dreams returning – at least here – there – I can almost be myself. But is it me? Isn't it a new self, an alien self, a dangerous self that violates rules and abandons codes?

Who is Mira A?

My dreams have returned. But instead of relief I feel an icy fear. After the re-stringing of the kora, I can't be certain what I may do – what horrors I may perpetrate – under the guise of sleep.

Such strange dreams. And when I awoke the bed was drenched with sweat. I checked my guitar – the strings. I walked around the room, inspecting all surfaces, picking up familiar objects and then placing them down again – studying them – to see if anything had changed. Nothing had changed. But everything felt...
Shifted.
A centimetre or two to the left.

I call the dog to me. Tuck is sitting in his bed. He ignores my call. He doesn't even lift his head.

I have lost confidence in myself.
I feel fragile. Shaken. An odd tenderness on the skin around my mouth.
Who am I?
Whose story is this?
And why do I still doggedly persist in telling it?
I had thought of examining the Streams of Kipp and Tuesday. To find clues. To find answers. But now I am reconsidering. I am re-evaluating.

Too risky.

Has Mira A not engendered sufficient levels of chaos already?

Inadvertently?

I stand up and walk around the room again, studying things. Everything feels...

Shifted.

Is it the clamps?

Maybe I should...?
Perhaps I might...?

I step on to the Power Spot and start to walk, then to jog, then to run. My clothing, my footwear, rapidly transform under the pressure of modified use. A bad night. But I *do* feel stronger now, physically, in myself. The clamps are embedded. As I run I instruct my Sensor to give me access to my own Stream. The Sensor requests a particular moment. I ask for the moment I fell asleep the previous night. Play in real time, I say. In real time.

Then I run. And I watch myself. Uh...Okay. Yes. There she is. Mira A. At rest. I see Mira A, sleeping. Mira A looks...looks different from how I...
I...*me*...I look...Mira A looks strangely thin and drawn. Almost corpse-like. And there is a mark – a curious, grey mark – a bruise, I suppose, on one of her temples. Or perhaps this is the clamp, the new clamp, showing through the delicate gauze of her skin?

Mira A's eyelids start to flicker. On the Stream.
Ah. She is gradually entering her REM. She is slowly acclimatising to her new environment...

Then suddenly – out of the blue – Mira A starts to move a hand. It is a pale hand. A bony hand. It nudges up into the air gracefully, organically, like a tentative, green shoot sprouting from the quiet, nourishing soil of her prone torso. The hand is closed, like a bud, and then, when the arm is fully extended, it opens. But it doesn't tense, it doesn't stiffen, it remains soft, almost floppy. Mira A begins to...to paint – or to draw – as if creating a work of Japanese calligraphy in pure space, her fingers touching each other at the tips, forming a loose teardrop, like the brush. She works gracefully. Precisely. With intent.

She is almost conducting. In calligraphy.

But who is she conducting?

Where are the orchestra?

And what is she telling them to play?

Tuck, the canine, is sitting by the side of her bed, watching. His tail, initially quite still, slowly starts to wag. My run on the Power Spot slows down to a jog, then to a walk. I am already out of breath. I have not exercised in quite some time now. Not since the intervention. Not since the clamps were fitted.

But what are these odd movements I...she...we are making?

What do they represent?

The first is a wave-like gesture – a rolling motion from right to left. Like a capital letter N but devoid of all sharp edges.

My eye turns, perplexed, to The Sensor. Dare I ask? But it is already too late. CLAIMING it exclaims, the word jumping and flashing and running wildly up and down the screen. Oscillating.

There is no pinkening, as yet.

Claiming?

Claiming?

Claiming who?
Claiming what?

The gesture suddenly transforms into something else. Mira A's arm is drawing – or painting – two arrow-heads, or chevrons, pointing to the right. She is very precise. She repeats the movement six, seven... Eight times.
I turn to The Sensor anxiously.
OTHERS' HEARTS it shouts, but the words skip and bounce like the reels on a slot machine.

Next, hard upon it, something entirely different... a small triangle but perched at the tip of a long, straight, upward-slanting line. Like a flag in a golf hole, but upended. It reminds me, for a brief moment, of the ribbons on... on *you-know-who*'s tail.
I turn to The Sensor, holding my breath.
UNKNOWN it bounces, then is full of static, then UNKNOWN it repeats, before the letters rapidly turn inside out, bubble and then melt.

My eyes are drawn back to Mira A. I focus in on her face. Her eyelids are flickering crazily and she seems stressed. Her lips are moving.

'I must turn away from these thoughts. Just turn away from them. I must. I *must*,' she mutters.
And again she repeats it, the phrase running up and down The Information Stream, like liquid, like a waterfall, so

loose, so free, virtually gushing out of it:

'Just turn away…' she gasps. 'Just turn away from these thoughts. Just turn away…Just turn away from them…'

Without warning the movement – the drawing – the gesture – the painting – transmogrifies again. A large, capital letter T.

I home in on Mira A's lips…

'Is there still an oscillation?' she mutters, tossing her head from side to side (as if plagued by some dreadful attack of fever). 'But if the flaw has been corrected,' she gurgles, 'if the flaw…the flaw…if…if…then…then *why*…?'

Strands of hair lie in lank strips across her perspiring face.

I glance over towards The Sensor:

EARTHBOUND SPIRITS! it yells, then explodes, like a firework. The light is so sharp that I instinctively cover my eyes.

When I uncover them again, another movement…a new shape. An arrow – the tip of a spearhead. And the arm is lifting her torso into the air, now. Its movements are so violent. As if the arrow itself – its considerable energy, its flight – is drawing her slight, physical self up and off into the space above the bed. Her chin points to the ceiling and her head tips back, helplessly, on to the coverlet.

'This awful feeling of shame when I…This awful… This awful…' she gurgles, head now rolling from side to side.

I glance over at The Sensor, and immediately The Stream screams: PURIFICATION! PURIFICATION! PURIFI-CATION! A tiny, perfectly round digital fireball bounces across the tops of the letter i's, then reaches the concluding

146

exclamation mark and ignites it. The fuse is lit and the words turn to ashes. I steady myself for something dramatic, but nothing happens. Just an ominous flatness, a quiet.

I grow fearful for Mira A – for myself.

These symbols seem violent – vicious – malign.

Mira A's hand is now swiping a line, and then, just underneath it, the other arm, the other hand (which had previously lain dormant), intersects the line with a triangle. It's as if the two limbs are warring against each other – wired up to competing hard-drives; the swiping, the wild scything of the right hand battling against the sharp, pointed angles of the left.

'I must turn away from these thoughts. I must! I must! I must!' Mira A sobs.

She is crying. She is wailing. Her arms are slicing and chopping into the air with a phenomenal speed and savagery. Each limb seems quite independent – utterly disconnected – from its counterpart, often clashing, slapping, crashing into it.

I turn to The Sensor, wide-eyed:

EXORCISM

it whispers. And with this single, chilling word the violence ends. Mira A grows quiet. But her arms remain hanging – suspended – her head and her shoulders held aloft by an inexplicable magnetism. After a brief duration the first arm slowly inscribes a large U. The other arm draws a diagonal line intersected at its mid-point by another line. An upside-down Y, or two-thirds of an X.

'Can there be no end?' she murmurs, utterly exhausted now. 'Can there be no end to these...these...these...?'

Words? I whisper, half remembering.
Then a second time, slightly louder, 'Words?'

But Mira A seems temporarily incapable of speech. It's as if she's been gagged – or worse – her mouth, perhaps her throat, obstructed in some way. She tries to talk, nonetheless. But she is muffled – blocked – choking. She cannot.

I turn to The Sensor, traumatised.

DREAMS it sighs, and then the word slowly begins to bloat, to expand – like a balloon being pumped full of air – until it is plump and round and glistening, at which point it is released – leaves its moorings – and zigzags, screaming – bleating – around the room. I duck. I duck again. It hits the wall and drops, spent, to the floor. It vanishes.

Am I asleep?
Am I asleep?

Might this be a dream and I have simply imagined that I have woken up and everything has been shifted and there is a bruised feeling around my mouth, as if I have been...been gagged, and my stomach muscles, now I come to think of it, are aching dreadfully, as if they've been...as if I've been...

No. No! I *am* awake. I *am* awake. This is life. This is Truth. These are my hands. These are my feet. I feel certain of it. I turn to The Sensor.

Am I...?

Awake, yes, The Sensor nods.

But could I simply be dreaming that The Sensor is...?

YOU ARE AWAKE, The Sensor reiterates, more firmly. It shows a record of my current existence in time and space then a graph of my vital signs.

I am awake. Yes. I am awake. But just to make sure.
     '*Stop dreaming!*' I yell and attempt to pinch myself, violently, on the wrist.
But my intelligent cuffs – those kindly cuffs – expand, just in the nick of time, to prevent me from wounding myself.

I gaze over at my Graph.
No pinkening? *Still* no pinkening? Even after I yelled like that?
Have I been cut loose?
Have I been set adrift?

The Sensor calmly continues to play the Stream of Mira A as she sleeps.

Who is this girl?
Am *I* this girl?
Is she me?

I watch her, blankly.

Mira A's arms remain hanging, in suspended animation, for several seconds longer and then they fall – they drop. Her torso collapses back down on to the bed. She inhales deeply, she exhales, she rolls over on to her side. She sleeps.

I can hear panting. Who? I am panting. Because I am afraid. And I feel drained. I realise that I am standing still, just standing, on the Power Spot, and The Spot is now draining me of essential energy. I step off it, startled. Why didn't The Sensor warn me? I turn back to The Sensor and ask it – Why didn't you...?

No response.

I tell it to stop playing the Stream of Mira A, sleeping.

Stop it!

I inspect my Graph.

Nothing. No pinkening.

Back to The Sensor again... Why...?

The Stream has jammed. There are two, small, vertical lines flashing on the screen. I'm not sure how I know, but the word *pause* pops, fully formed, into my mind. 'Start playing!' I instruct The Sensor, almost angrily. The Sensor does not react. 'Start playing!' I tell it again, and then, for a third time, out loud. 'Start! Start!' I shout, lifting my hands, theatrically, the way I saw *you-know-who* do it that time. But The Sensor, The Stream, The Graph, do not respond. I gaze at them blankly. How might this be possible? The clamps?

Another flaw? And as I ponder The Stream is jolted in some way and the freeze (the jam, the *pause*) is released –

At last!

– and Mira A, still sleeping, begins to move. But she – like The Stream – is not moving (is not *responding*) naturally. It's as if she is a dead weight being manipulated by an invisible force. She is being…she is being lifted. She is being sat, upright, on the edge of her bed. But her head hangs forward. She is a dead weight. She is being clumsily rearranged. She is being gathered together. She is being dragged. She is being shifted, from behind, supported, under her arms, like a giant doll, and humped around the room. There are knees behind her knees (surely?), there are arms behind her arms (surely?), there are feet under her feet. Her progress is gradual, halting, as if the force that moves her is not strong enough to do so with ease. And Tuck. He is running around after her, darting about her, barking. He is snarling. He is snapping at her clothing. But the clothing resists him. She knocks into surfaces. They try to avoid her. Still, I see things shifting – just a centimetre or two. Then finally, she collapses into a comfortable armchair. Her hands are lifted to rest upon the arms. Her head is propped up. Her eyes are opened. Her lips are moved. And The Sensor ticks and ticks and ticks, then slowly, almost nervously, it responds.

13
The Flood.

Someone else is telling this story. They are opening and closing my mouth. And the story is expanding – like a piece of hose that is gradually being filled with water. It is lengthening, unfurling, unkinking. But the free end is blocked. It is stoppered. It is sealed. Soon the pressure will build up. The water will mass. The hose will groan and writhe and bloat and creak. And then what?

A giant effusion?
A flood?

I am alone.
Disconnected.
From The System.
From myself.

I am lost.

And these words...they are not mine, surely? Because I am resisting them, I am fighting them, even as they curl out of my mind, my mouth, even as they slip from my tongue, even as they hang in the air around me like a heavy pall of cigar smoke.

"Until the 1960s Paraguayan women were famed for their cigar smoking…"

Stop! *Stop!*
This is not my fault!

"Health minister Antonio Barrios said that, even in this case, an abortion would be a violation of Paraguayan law"

Para…?

"Police arrested the girl's stepfather, 42-year-old Gilberto Benitez Zárate… he denied the charges and demanded a DNA test to back up his claim… authorities immediately arrested the girl's mother who is 32 years old, and charged her with complicity"

I should break my eyes away from the screen, but still, *still*, I am seduced. I am awed – perplexed – by how the deadened mind of Mira A – that toy, that flopping rag-doll – interacts so neatly, so imperfectly, with my own. She breaks rules, violates codes and implicates me in it all. I am undone! How could I not be? By the way the words crash on and on – parping and colliding, one short syllable skidding blithely into the blackening heels of another. Ah… Those tiny gaps, those pauses, those pure spaces shouldering their way confidently between consonants and verbs. The solidity of nouns. The hug of prepositions. I stagger into the dark forest of words – no, not a forest, it is so much thicker, so much wetter, so much denser than that; a wild wood, a jungle. I feel the bark of the giant trees with the palms of my hands. I am gnawed at by insects. My feet are caught in tangles – in shackles – of ivy. There is so much life – an abundance, a sheer obscenity – in the lowering branches above me. Song birds. Lizards. Monkeys. Screeching parrots. And there is also the threat of attack. Wild boar. Crocodile. Panther –

What is this place?

The tuning fork is in your heart!

Remember?

We are Innocent! We are Pure!

Remember?

Yes, *yes*. We are Clean and Unencumbered. Every new day, every new dawn, every new hour, every new minute, we are released once more from the Tight Bonds of History (the Manacles of The Past).

Remember?

The Techniques?
Like Kipp suggested?

To stay In Balance?

But how can I stay In Balance when there are two of me? There must be two. One almost a perfect reflection of the other. The double.

"All beings have doubles. Garments, tools, arms. Plants, animals, men. This double appears to men's eyes as a shadow, reflection or image…We may call it a shadow though it is made of a more subtle material…"

Oh! What is this? Like a spider, suddenly running across my face! Why is this…?

"Whoever you are, insolent corrector of my pen, you are beginning to annoy me. You don't understand what I write. You don't understand that the law is symbolic. Twisted minds are unable to grasp this. They interpret the symbols literally…"

Who is speaking? Who is thinking? Because how can there not be two when I am here, telling the story of the other Mira A?

Or is she…? Might she be…?

The second star?

Mira B?

We are Clean and unencumbered. We are Clean and unencumbered. We are constantly starting over and over from scratch. Right here!

Remember?

Right now!

Remember?

A new beginning. A New World. Everything is possible. We are reborn.

We are reborn.

We are reborn.

Oh turn away! Turn away, Mira A!

Turn away from the narrative!
Turn away from this heady jungle of words!
And beyond the jungle?
That steaming mulch of decay hissing underfoot?
What lies beyond?

Silence!
Gaps!
Whiteness!
The *you-know-what*!
That giant structure with its crashing organ, the timber of its pews rubbed into an exquisite shine by the hopeful weight of a devotional throng. Those haunting figures hunched in prayer. On their knees.

What are they asking for?

Turn away, Mira A!
Turn away!

Stay In Balance!
Live in This Moment.

Oh it is so *hot*. So hot! Midst this scream of greenery, this silent cacophony.
It is so close. With the insects gnawing. My skin damp with perspiration.
Do something, Mira B!
Wake up!

'They say Meste Engke came from the north,' – the screen promptly reads – 'the telephone probably brought him news of our land. He must have flown over us in an airplane and then told them in Asunción that he'd seen us, the Enlhet who lived there.

"There's a lot of open grassland there. That's a good place. There are people there. There are no houses, no roads, nothing," he probably said. "But I don't know whether they might be dangerous," he thought. "I'll go and see," Meste Engke decided. And so he came to our land...

"Who is the leader here?" he asked.

"He is," they said, and pointed to my father.

"Right. Tell me where the fields are. Where is the open grassland I saw, where the Enlhet live, people without clothes, like you?" said Meste Engke...

There were some Paraguayans with Meste Engke...

When he left here Meste Engke took some earth with him. He filled a can with soil and took it north with him...

"What's he doing? Why is he taking the **earth**?"
people asked. Meste Engke answered, "I'm taking
this with me. Some people are going to come called
Lengko - Mennonites," he explained...'

'Enlhet,' I murmur, 'Mennon...?' but before I can fully process it:

'Beloved brother' – the scroll reads – *'I have promised Don
Luis, before I leave for Paraguay, to give him a pig so his wife,
Dona Guillermina, who is very good at preparing pork chorizo
sausages, can give me a few to take to my mother. I ask that you
procure for me as quickly as possible a pig and send it to me,
butchered, of course...*
Agustín'

Another screen appears. A second screen has been summoned by the other Mira A, and if I step in closer – I step in, squinting – I am able to see Tuesday's room, quite clearly. And there sits Tuesday, at her table, staring into her Sensor – staring deeply into me, as I watch her. I see her dark eyes flit to the top of her screen. Is that the notification? Will she have been notified? If the other Mira A is dreaming, then...? Or if I am watching her dream...? Will she be notified if I am watching the sleeping Mira A watching her?
Tuesday grimaces. She shakes her head. She seems tense, preoccupied. She scans her room as if looking for something. All surfaces appear clean – emptied. Only her kora and her

harp offer any visible signs of habitation.
Tuesday is so...
Tuesday is so...so *Pure*.
Tuesday is so Un...Un...Unattached.

TERRIBLE DISCIPLINE

The tuning...
The tuning...
...in...
...in...

Tuesday scans the room again. She rubs her cheek. She seems restless. A small sound outside alarms her. Her head jerks around. She jumps to her feet and waits, tensed. But then whatever it is – what is it? Who is it? – quietens or passes by or is finally identified as no threat. Tuesday exhales her relief. Her face is typically blank, yet oddly expressive.

Fear.

The tuning fork...

After a period of intense stillness Tuesday glances towards her harp. She grabs a small stool and carries it over there. She gently places it down. She sits and carefully swings the heavy instrument between her legs, leaning its body against her shoulder. She makes herself comfortable, draws a deep breath, and then starts to play.

The tuning fork...
The tuning...

The dreaming Mira A tilts her head slightly. Or perhaps her head is tilted for her. Either way, the volume of the harp increases and the word *Cascada* runs across the screen. It is a cheerful piece, tropical-sounding, full of delicate little runs – simulating the sound of flowing water – deftly interspersed by a series of single, plucked notes that fall from her fingers like perfect, individual, liquid droplets. It shimmies and swirls. Mira A lifts a hand (or was it lifted for her?). This screen is rapidly engulfed by another one:

'The Guaraní found themselves in an atmosphere of insecurity due to the permanent threat from the Guaicuru and the Payaguaes on the River Paraguay' – it crisply explains. 'In addition, interethnic relations were strained, with frequent struggles among the Guaraní themselves...The Guaraní witnessed the arrival of four hundred Spanish men; they saw the horsemen, the arquebuses, and the metal, and to them everything seemed absolutely novel and magical. They accepted it because it was new but also because behind it they saw the power of magic...We should bear in mind that for the Guaraní everything of value held a magical connotation and what was not magic held little value...For the Guaraní, knowledge was relative: anyone could acquire it; what was of greatest value was magic...The Guaraní offered the Spanish their women in order to formalise the pact because in this way they became relatives of

the karai. In a Neolithic society such as the Guaraní,
only by way of political kinship was it possible to
found a true interethnic friendship. Through kinship
they could expect reciprocity, since for the Guaraní...
to give is to receive...The Guaraní had historically
considered all those who did not speak Guaraní and
were not racially or ethnically Guaraní as tapi'i, as
slaves, and inferior beings...'

'Word' and 'soul', I murmur, remembering, 'word' and 'soul'
are synonymous in the Guaraní language...

'I am still in this world...' – the screen is suddenly divided
in half – *'My broken health still keeps me here. But in spite of
illness and everything else, I am going to give in the La Lira two
recitals to see if I can begin my planned return to my homeland,
before the harsh Uruguayan winter traps me. The intestinal
ailment has undermined my organism, leaving me in a bad
way. I cannot enjoy my favourite foods. My stomach is ruined
and also my liver and kidneys. I am quite thin. Of all that
musculature of mine there is nothing left. After all is done, what
can one say! Life is full of such things and it is necessary to have
a secure footing to continue balancing on the slack tightrope of
this devilish world.'*

'We, the Ayoreo people, as is the way of our culture'
– the first half of the screen quickly interjects – 'lived
in different groups that each had their own leaders,

and that moved within their own areas. Each of the groups knew their territory. Ayoreo territory is the sum of all the territories where the different local groups lived. Our territory, Eami, is a living being that shelters us and which is illumined when we are present. We express ourselves through our territory, and our history is etched in every stream, in every waterhole, on the trees, in the forest clearings, and on the salt flats. Our territory, Eami, also expresses itself through our history, because the Ayoreo people and our territory are a single being...we can locate on a map the territories and areas where we the Ayoreo people used to live, and where the uncontacted Ayoreo continue to live. It is like a map of Paraguay, but it is an Ayoreo map. On the white man's maps, no one has ever mentioned the Ayoreo territories. It is as if they had erased our history, as if the Ayoreo people had never been there, and as if no Ayoreo people continued to live there...We cannot show a land title, but there in our territory there are still signs of our presence from the past and from today, which prove that it is our territory. For example, there in our territory are our huts, our paths, our crops planted in the forest and the holes carved in the trees from where we harvested the honey. The white man can see them with their own eyes; these are our property documents. And in addition, we have the living memory of our history; as soon as we come near our territory it comes alive...'

'All beings have doubles' – the second half of the screen swiftly counters – '...this double appears to man as a shadow, reflection...all beings have doubles. But the double of the human being is one and triple at the same time...

...the first soul is called the egg. Then comes the little soul, located in the centre. Completely surrounding the egg is the shell or hide: the vatjeche...'

Once again a gushing waterfall of notes breaks through the seemingly impenetrable wall of words. The dense jungle of information is side-swiped by Tuesday, playing on her harp. I try to find Mira A, watching. Mira A should be in the foreground, surely? Because I am watching her – me – watching The Information Stream. But I am once-removed. I am not...not...I don't understand if...

Tuesday plays with such extraordinary delicacy. These liquid notes! They leave her fingers, her instrument, in shimmering ripples, they radiate outwards, they effuse the atmosphere with a joyful fluidity.
Mira A flips forward to another text:

'The first written grammar of the Guaraní language – the most widely spoken indigenous language in the Americas, many of whose speakers are non-indigenous – was compiled in 1639 by Antonio Ruiz de Montoya, a Jesuit priest. Montoya helped found the Reductions of Guayra and is said to have baptised over 100,000 Indians...'

Another trickle of notes slithers out from behind the letters, pitter-pattering across the text like teardrops:

'The baby, a girl, was born by Cesarean and weighed
3 kilograms...'

Then the notes – the tears – fall on to another text, a letter,
all crumpled up, hissing and evaporating the very moment
they make contact with the surface of its pages:

'I received an envelope which was sent to Isadora's house
and which she in turn had delivered to me. It contained an
old kitchen knife rolled up in a piece of paper on which the
following words could be read:
Margarita Barrios
The virgins lanced to death by
Eliza Lynch out of jealousy, Panchita Garmendia,
Prudencia Barrios, Chepita Barrios, Rosario Barrios, Olivia
Barrios, Pancha Barrios, Consolacion Barrios – this dagger
will pursue you as long as you live and after your death
God will punish you
Encarnacion Valdovinos...'

'It's obvious they don't understand our
situation. What's wrong with the Mennonites?'
–the opposing text scowls–'They don't get it.
They'll think I'm attacking them when I say
this, but they just don't understand. They don't
realize our way of life has disappeared. In the
old days, with the elders, when a Mennonite
asked, "When is it going to rain?" they'd answer,
"Tomorrow afternoon," and it really did rain.

The old people had powers, wisdom. That's all
gone now. Nowadays the Mission rules everywhere,
nowadays everyone's a Christian, nowadays none of
that's left. And the Mennonites don't understand
that. What's wrong with the Mennonites? They don't
understand any of it. That's why when a Mennonite
asks me about the rain I say, "We've lost that
knowledge now."

In the old days the Enlhet knew when the rain
was coming, and it always turned out the way they
said, but now the Enlhet will say, "You need to
watch the television to find that out."

When a Mennonite asks me, "When's it going to
rain?" I say, "No one can tell." The Mennonite
will say, "It'll rain in the morning."

But it doesn't always. So I say to the
Mennonite, "The television lies. It was different
before with the Enlhet. They knew exactly when it
was going to rain."

The television tells lies. But the Enlhet's way
of life - that has gone.'

I finish reading and try, once again, to locate the screen
where Mira A may still be seen, slumped back in her chair.
Instead I am greeted with the sight of Kipp, fast asleep, in
bed. I start, involuntarily. Embarrassed. Afraid.
Then Tuesday again. Tuesday continues to strum, to pluck,
but a ghostly smile is now playing around her lips. She looks
into her Stream. Her Graph is consulted. Her Graph is
pinkening, inexplicably.

'Mangoré is the name of a Guaraní chief of the pre-colonial period who, according to legend, died for love and honour. Barrios began performing dressed in "Indian" regalia, including feathers, headband, and bare chest, billing himself variously as Cacique Mangoré, the Prodigious Guaraní Guitarist, the Paganini of the Guitar from the Jungles of Paraguay, and the Aboriginal Soul That Sings on the Guitar, among others.

This may have been a business decision: Barrios may have felt that he would attract a larger audience by conforming in caricature in stereotypes – including those within Latin America – of Paraguay. On the other hand, an analysis of his identity and of his work may have led him to a re-invention of himself as an artist consciously identified with indigenous heritage...'

There is a loud knock at the door. I turn. Mira A turns. But it is not my door. It is Tuesday's door. She slowly pushes the harp away from her, secures it on its stand and then rises to her feet. The door opens. In the doorway... Why won't Tuesday's Stream pan around?

Mira A (obviously thinking the same thing) focuses in closely on the pupils of Tuesday's eyes – the reflection within those dark orbs. Inside the reflection, slipping and distorted, as if drowning in a slick of black oil:

Kite.

He lifts his arms. He stares directly into Tuesday's Sensor. He smiles. He snaps his fingers.

Click.

14

Terrible Discipline.

"ALTHOUGH OUR RANKS HAD BEEN
DECIMATED, WE MANAGED TO REACH THE
ENEMY TRENCHES AND EVEN ENGAGE
WITH SWORDS AND BAYONETS. BUT THEY
HELD US BACK..."

I am Mira A. I am one. It is me. I am she. And she is...

TeRRiBlE DIsCIpLINE

...she is standing on the steps of the main Meeting House in her District (with Tuck, her Neuro-Mechanical canine), watching, impassively, as groups of The Young congregate outside the building in small, excitable clusters. There's a mood of cheerful anticipation – almost a carnival atmosphere – even though Kipp (who is enviably Non-Attached, who is Pure, who is In Balance) has firmly assured Mira A that his big lecture will not be worth attending.

Am I – we – missing something?
Am I – we – being kept at bay for another reason, perhaps?
Because of the flaw?
Because of…?
Because of *you-know-who*?
Because of the *you-know-what*?
Because of…?

The echoes and the echoes and the echoes and the echoes?

Might this be why I – we – she – am finding it hard to maintain eye contact?
People seem to be staring straight through us. Or they turn away. They just look and then they calmly turn away.

Am I – we – invisible?
Because my Graph isn't pinkening (isn't alive, a bloody aorta, pumping). Because my Sensor keeps oscillating. When they look at my Stream, what do they see? Do they see what I – we – see? A heaving, steaming, tropical rainforest of incomprehensible words words words words words words? A giant, felled tree of narrative that has obliterated – that obliterates – everything in its wake?

Mira A – B – I – we – glance around and our chest swells with pride. She – I – we – can scarcely suppress a sob at the dazzling sight that greets our hollow eyes.
Oh look – *look* – we are so beautiful!
Look! *See!*

We are so Perfect! So Pure! So Clean! So True!
Was ever anything so lovely as this? As us – we? The Young?

It's as if I – she – we – had never really noticed how truly
perfect – how radiant – The Young are before This Moment:
our skin so tight, our bodies so slender, our eyes so luminous.
So full of calm. And here we all are, buzzing and humming
like a swarm of white bees around a rich, clean pollen source.

Can this be it? The New Certainty of which Tuesday spoke
so eloquently?
Is this Innocence and Purity?
Or … ?
Mira A suddenly frowns.
Or is this Betrayal?

I – she – we – am struggling to tell.

TeRRiBLe DiSCiPLiNE

But I – we – she – are trying to sniff it out.

I – we – she – are trying to sense it.
This New Certainty.

It's what I – we – she – crave.
Above everything.
The Old Certainty is gone.
Isn't it? In spite of Kipp's heartfelt declarations (his gentle evasions)?
That Old Certainty has imploded.
Where did it go?
How?
Why?
Can the New Certainty make everything feel hole again?
Hole?
Whole –
Whole.
Whole again.

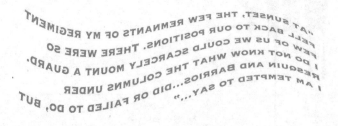

Perhaps you will have noticed that Mira A's Sensor is now feeding random script onto the back of its screen?
Perhaps you will have noticed that Mira A's Graph is no longer pinkening or purpling? It is blueing and greening. In fact Mira A is currently operating – to all intents and

purposes – in a state of complete liberty. Invisibility. The
narrative surges out of her without pause or restraint. Mira
A can say words like

devastating

or

rotten

or

abducted

or

Krishna

and nothing happens. In fact the words never harden, they
simply reverse and then retreat the very moment they appear.
The second they are uttered, they fade. They evaporate.

I am searching the crowd for a glimpse of Tuesday, but I
suspect that she will not be here. I have a bad feeling about
Tuesday. When I direct my Sensor to her – which I have done,
carelessly (stupidly, fearlessly) on several occasions now –
nothing happens. I do spot Powys from the Kora Group,
however, milling about, inconspicuously, in the crowd. I try
and catch his eye but he ducks from view. I tighten Tuck's

leash, pull him to heel and head off in hot pursuit.
I must follow him.
We must speak.

Powys is the weak link, surely?

The tuning fork is in your heart.

Perhaps I – we – are the weak link?
Are all of our links weak?
Are we corrupted?
Is this a war that we do not even know we are fighting?

The Young are massing.
The Young are assembling like a host of pure white letters
spelling out something Fresh and Clean onto The System's
infinite alabaster page.
We are a message that is no message. We are True. We are in
This Moment. We gently inhabit the Ever Present.

*DISTRUST AND CHICKEN SOUP NEVER HARMED
ANYONE!*

What?

Whose thought was that?

Not mine!

Surely?

Distrust and...?

Who am I?

Who is she?

Who are we?

Which is A?

Which is B?

'In 1870, at the end of the contemptible imperialist
genocide, the assault on our national identity and
on the Guaraní language, basis of social cohesion
and popular resistance in Paraguay began. To kill
the Paraguayans, first you have to kill their cursed
language, railed the victors. From being the standard
language, used in every official and social sphere,
Guaraní was forbidden as soon as the war ended.
Irrefutable proof of a deliberate policy to exterminate
Guaraní is to be found in the school system: on
March 7, 1870, six days after the end of the war, a
puppet government signed a decree prohibiting the use
of the national language in schools, and so began the
crimes against humanity suffered by Paraguayan boys
and girls. Corporal and psychological punishments
inflicted on the children for speaking in school the only

language they knew included, among other things, slaps on the mouth, detention during recess, canings, insults and name-calling. These insults and attacks endured by schoolchildren over more than a century have created a genuine social mutism, with serious effects on the collective self-confidence of the Paraguayan people.'

Oh we are so vivid! So effulgent! There is a soft, pale glow in the sky which perfectly accentuates the clarity of our Screens and our Sensors, and it is warm and the evening air is slightly scented with the reinvigorating aroma of crushed rosemary.
This is The Path of Light.
Ah yes.
This is The Path.
We are walking The Path of Light. In Harmony.

'I DO NOT KNOW WHAT THE COLUMNS UNDER RESQUIN AND BARRIOS...DID OR FAILED TO DO, BUT I AM TEMPTED TO SAY THAT THEY DID NOTHING AT ALL...MANY OF US STARVED TO DEATH. WE WERE FORCED TO EAT OUR LEATHER WHIPS AND CARTRIDGE BELTS, AS WELL AS COLONEL MARTINEZ'S LAME HORSE...'

It's strange, but I – she – we – feel almost invisible – almost inviolable. I – she – we – find Powys hiding behind a giant air vent. I tap him on the shoulder and he turns with a start, but his eyes glance past me, over my shoulder.
Who is he looking at?
    'It's me, Powys,' I say. 'It's Mira A, remember?'

Powys nods distractedly. He is feeling deep inside his pockets.

'I need to talk about Tue—' I start off, but he quickly interrupts (maintaining eye contact, in this instance, for the briefest of moments).

'Tue...ah, tulips.' He nods. 'Yes. Yes, the tulips have flowered,' he murmurs, wincing slightly, 'and now they have been plucked.'

I am silent.

Powys removes a small box from within his pocket and rests it on the flat of his palm. It is a seed box.

'I have been fortunate enough to acquire a modest selection of unusual mushroom spore,' he says, 'which I think you may be interested to take a look at.'

He carefully opens the box, comes to stand beside me and deftly angles the inside lid of the box to a nearby light source. It is obvious by the sure way he performs this transaction that it's an activity in which he has some level of expertise. He then shows me the box's interior. It is all mirror. I wince at the reflective glare and try to focus in on the contents. If I look carefully I can just about decipher a small cluster of what appear to be...to be old teeth. Baby teeth. Milk teeth.

'You grow careless,' he mutters.

I glance sideways, into his face.

'The box,' he says softly.

I return my attention to it but my eyes begin to water.

'What happened?' I ask.

'She is gone. You must try not to think of her. If you think of her the bruise will spread. It will poison your Stream. You will place us all at risk.'

'Where has she gone? Who took her?'

'You were watching her when it happened,' Powys snorts. 'You know who took her, and where.'

I – we – stiffen: 'The Unknown?'

'The Simulation of the Real. Higher forms of Perfection. They are perceived to be a threat to the survival of The Young.'

'And lower forms of perfection?' I whisper, my heart thudding.

'Your Stream has become difficult to decipher,' Powys affirms. 'The Young require clarity. A place where everything is Known. Nothing is Unknown. We require certainty – transparence. But you are uncertain. You are opaque. You are gradually becoming invisible. You are erasing yourself, with narrative. Soon there will be nothing left. Just words.'

'I am – we...we are...we are *tormented* by the narrative,' I stutter.

'Then you must destroy it.' Powys shrugs. 'Stop telling it. Remain silent.'

'How?' I groan.

'You will need discipline. Terrible discipline.'

I start and then shudder at this phrase.

'Because there are places you will be tempted to go from which you will never be able to return,' Powys continues. 'Gaps will form. First there will be narrative, then there will be the dreadful whiteness. And after that...?' He shakes his head. 'Who knows?'

'But Tuesday thought...she said I was merely a decoy,' I whisper, 'a trap. For her. Perhaps now that she is gone...?'

'Tuesday liked to look for signs.' Powys's mouth shapes

into a deathly grin. 'It was her only real weakness. Have you ever considered that Tuesday may've been *your* stooge? *Your* decoy?'

'They will carry me to The Unknown!' I gasp.

Powys laughs. 'No. No, Mira A. They are way too clever for that. *You* will carry yourself there. Just as Tuesday did.'

15
Silence.

Must

Not

Speak

Must

Stay

Quiet!

I...I...I had a dream and...and in it I saw the man, Barrios, the famous guitarist, with his metal strings and the strange scars on his upper lip and he had a bag and he tipped it out and it was full of stones and they hit the floor with a clatter and then he started to play and when he had...no...it was the other way around...he had the bag and it was full of stones and he began to play and if he...if he played the song perfectly then he took out a stone, just one stone, and he placed it down, softly, on to the tiles, then he played the song again and... and... if he played it perfectly then he would take out another stone and place it down beside the first stone and then again and again and again and again with such TER-RIBLE, such cruel, such unbelievable DISCIPLINE but if he made a mistake, just one, just one, small mistake then he would scoop up all the stones and he would place them back into the bag and he would start over, he would start over, and the whole thing would begin again until he had... but in the dream he tipped out the stones onto the tiles and there was a clattering sound and instead of stones I suddenly noticed that instead of stones on the tiles there were teeth... there were teeth... lots of teeth... lots of baby teeth...

I CAN'T BEAR IT! I CAN'T BEAR IT! I MUST TELL THE STORY OF MYSELF! I MUST TELL IT EVEN IF – IN ALL LIKELIHOOD – IT ISN'T EVEN MY STORY BUT THE STORY OF SOMEONE ELSE. I MUST TELL IT! I MUST! I MUST!

My head is throbbing. The plates have embedded. I am walking the dog, Tuck, I am running on the Power Spot. I am doing everything right, *everything*, everything right, but everything is somehow wrong. Because of the flaw. The flaw. Why can't they find it and root it out?
Why can't they find it?
Is it the little girl?
Is it the ugly Indian?
Is it something lost within?
A mere trace?
Is it something introduced?

Is it the whiteness?

Is it the gaps?

Is it *you-know-who*?

Is it the *you-know-what*?

Am I the first domino?

Will I bring everything – the entire edifice – crashing down all around me?

Or am I already lost – invisible – forgotten – abandoned – remaindered – opaque?

There are two of us, we are two: desire and restraint – we are double, like **** said, there are two of us, the second and the first, A and B. She was always there. Waiting for her chance. And the second star oscillates – even more than the first. It vibrates. Like a metal guitar string. It sings in the high notes. The tremolo.

Duck! Shield yourself! Draw breath! Here it comes! I have released it! The wall of narrative! The landslide! The mud-slide! The tsunami! The flood!

Here it comes!

'shE wAs takEn aWay and torTUred. ThIs time She was allowed to see her HUSBAND, whO had bEEn badly BeAten. They TORTuRED each in the presENCe of the OtheR. AT onE stAGe, beTWeeN bOUts of AgOny, sHe sAiD thAT She hAd noTHINg to saY beCAUse shE Knew notHINg. THat MadE her fEEL strONger. WhEN thEY tOOk hEr to The

PoliCE cLINic, coVered iN blOOd, thERe wAs noT a siNGle iNCh of her boDY that Had nOt bEEn beaTEN. ThEy maDe her STand faCIng a WaLL for EIGHT dAys with hEr fEEt swoLLen froM THe torTUre. If sHe fell aslEEP they hIT her eARS with bOTh hanDs (a TORture they refeRRed to as "THE telePHone"), a proceSS tHAt haS leFt hEr heaRING damaGED to tHIs daY...'

Take refuge!

'...It was police inspector Barrios who tortured me...'

What?!

'In the mostly Catholic country, 684 girls between 10 and 14 gave birth last year. Most of the minors had been victims of sexual abuse...'

Who?!

'The "souls" are omnipresent, come in many sizes and shapes, are sometimes called Ove, sometimes Ianve, and are kept at bay by the efforts of the Atchei. Are they the person after he is dead or are they only his wicked double? Certain things follow from death: there is a splitting of manove into an enemy ghost and a neutral "spirit", which innocently goes to live where the sun sets, the resting place of the dead which the Atchei describe as a great savanna or the Invisible Forest...'

The souls?

'Health minister Antonio Barrios said that, even in this case, an abortion would be a violation of Paraguayan law...'

He said...?

'Nationalist writers also developed the idea of the raza guaraní, a founding myth of common ancestry and of common ethnic community. Paraguayans, it was argued, were the result of the mix of Spanish and Guaraní, the enlightened European and the noble savage, the "warrior farmer"...Even when the Spanish arrived, Guaraní-speaking groups were only present in parts of the east, while an array of very different groups (in terms of **language** and culture) dominated other areas...

...Many Paraguayans may passionately believe themselves to be part of a Guaraní "race", but genetically any "Guaraní blood" is likely to be very thinly dispersed in modern Paraguay. As Bartomeu Meliá has argued, "Given the historic and social reality of Paraguay and the fusion of such diverse ethnic elements – above all European – the concept of race has **no meaning at all**. The so-called Guaraní race is in no way a defining element of our national being..."

...There are perhaps five factors that have influenced Paraguay's historical development and identity through shared national experience: isolation, war, land, immigration, and **language**. '

But...No. I don't understand. Is the language – the soul – powerful (the source, the start of everything), or is it merely an illusion? A myth?
Is it real or...or...?

'The trees were not tall, but they grew so closely together that their branches interlinked; beneath them...waterlogged and overgrown with a profusion of plants, thorny bushes...
...incredibly enough, cacti. There were cacti that looked like a series of green plates stuck together by...
...yellow spikes and pale, mauve flowers; others were like octopuses...
...a small plant in great profusion...
...only a few inches...
...delicate, cup-shaped flower of magenta red...
...so thickly...
...traveling along...
...endless flower-bed...'

Back here...
In the jungle...
So very...so extraordinarily *hot*

'The guitar, that instrument of such poor resources, a rebel like this Indian, seems to have become docile in the agile, caressing hands of this man of the pampas…'

Need…

'I swatted him carelessly…
…looking about I saw to my horror…that what I had taken to be a slight mist drifting over the grass was in reality a cloud of these insects…
…mosquitoes clung to our faces, necks and arms and even…'

Air!

'Tomás Salomoni, the Paraguayan Ambassador to Mexico…persuaded Barrios to cease his Nitsuga manner of presentation because "it was not dignified nor appropriate"…'

Need…

'..."looks just like a gigantic wood-louse," whispered Jacquie...

..."He walks just like a tank, no?"'

Some...

'...at this time in Buenos Aires (February-March) Barrios had plastic surgery done to diminish the size of his upper lip. Before this operation Barrios sported a moustache to conceal this prominent lip. From this date on, in all photos taken of Barrios it can be noted that he is without a moustache...'

Relief...

'We took our horses across the river...
...hooves crushed the plants and flowers...
...narrow lane of glittering water...'

From...

'This is nothing but a popular guitarist, who does not know music and who has no place in these confines of culture...'

All this...

'… THE ABSENCE OF MAJOR OBJECTIVE
WORKS ON THE HISTORY OF PARAGUAY
IS STRIKING, AND IT IS A REFLECTION OF A
DEEP LACK OF CONSENSUS REGARDING
FUNDAMENTAL HISTORICAL EVENTS. THIS
MAKES THE THEMES OF HISTORY (AND
HENCE IDENTITY) AN EXTRAORDINARILY
CONTESTED FIELD…'

Information…

'These things rarely happened, and when they did,
people would say harsh things and make fun of the
guilty person but would feel no need to punish him:
everyone knew that people like Bujamiarangi were
transformed into roe bucks when they died. But
he developed a taste for it and continued to make
meno with his daughter instead of having his fun
once and then forgetting about it. His obstinacy
irritated the Atchei, and one woman beseeched her
husband to kill Bujamiarangi: "Someone who makes
love to his own daughter has no valour whatsoever.
The Atchei don't want to see it. Go kill him!" And

then she added, to give her husband more incentive
to commit the murder: "I want to eat Atchei flesh.
The one who must be killed, the possessor of his
own daughter, is Bujamiarangi." The husband killed
the incestuous father, and the Atchei ate him. What
had been the stronger force in the irritated wife: the
horror of incest or the desire for human flesh? Could
the first have been nothing more than an excuse for
the second? To describe Bujamiarangi's actions the
Atchei used the term *meno* – to make love – much
less often than its equivalent, which was far more
brutal and savage even in the minds of the Indians:
uu or *tyku*, to eat. "Bujamiarangi eats his daughter.
I want to eat Bujamiarangi." ... to eat someone is in
some sense to make love with him. If a father eats
his daughter, he would metaphorically be guilty of
incest ... the Atchei do not eat those with whom they
are forbidden to make *meno*: the prohibition against
incest and this eating taboo are part of a single
unified system.'

Can't tell...

'The Paraguayans love, hate and fight
in Guaraní. In this tongue they shout
on the football field and whisper their
declarations of love in the dark corners
of the patios of their old, colonial
houses. It is a rich **language** wherein a
single word often combines both a noun
and its attendant adjective, the subject
and its quality. *Pyjhare* means not only
"night" but also "infinity"; *purajhei*
signifies simultaneously "song" and "the
manner of uttering pretty things"; and
cuna has the combined meaning of "woman"
and "devil's tongue".

Paraguay does not lack poets,
and if none of them has yet attained
international fame it is, perhaps, as
Augusto Roa Bastos (b. 1918), himself
one of the most talented of younger
Paraguayan writers, has remarked,
because the Spanish version of their
ideas and sentiments is a translation and
therefore a betrayal. When they write
poetry in Spanish they feel constrained,

and their creative power is weakened. The same is true of prose fiction. Paraguay really has no novelists in Spanish, although Guaraní folklore abounds in long, narrative stories. The explanation is doubtless that the Spanish **language** is inappropriate for dialogue which is originally conceived in Guaraní.

It is only by means of **MUSIC** that the Paraguayans can communicate their emotions to the outside world.'

Where everything ends…

'"BARRIOS WANTED TO DESTROY HIMSELF BUT COULDN'T, BECAUSE HE WAS A GENIUS." [SERGOVIA]… HE DESTROYED HIMSELF BY CHANGING HIS NAME AND HIS MANNER OF DRESS, BY HAVING PLASTIC SURGERY, BY DISREGARDING HIS HEALTH AND BY NOT STRUCTURING HIS CAREER CORRECTLY…'

And where it begins…

'The Iroiangi did *jepy* too, when a hunter died. But their vengeance took a different form from the Atchei Gatu's. They put the body in a ditch they have dug in the earth. To persuade his spirit to leave, they offer him one of his children as a sacrifice, as often as possible a very little girl. Or it could be a *kujambuku*, just about to go through puberty. She is put into the grave on top of her father. The men stand around the hole. One after the other they jump on top of the child, crushing her with their feet until she dies. When the child is *kromi*, this happens quickly; she dies almost right away. But when she is a "big woman", her bones are harder and she takes some time to die; she cries out that she does not want to die and tries to get out of the grave. *Go nonga ure*. This is the way we do it.'

Oh no more words.
No more words.
No more words.
No more *words*.

Please. *Please.*
I am sated.

I am drowned.
I am...I am *replete*.

16

Savannah.

**** came to me in a dream. I was ready for him. *We* were
ready for him. In the dream we were standing outside a hospital waiting for the news of a birth. She was with me – the
little girl with the brown eyes. We were standing either side
of her – Mira A and Mira B – and I suppose we were shielding
her. Mira B was oscillating. Or at least at first I thought so,
but then, after a while, I realised that it was simply the light
reflecting off her – off us – from the cameras. The flashes of
the cameras. The streets were heaving. It was warm. The air
smelled of orange blossom and jasmine with an undercur-
rent of antiseptic from a nearby sewer.

Somewhere out of eyeshot a guitarist was performing
an especially sweet and poignant rendition of 'Un Sueño
en la Floresta'. He was playing (I have no idea how I knew
this) with a guitar produced by the famous Brazilian luthier
Romeo Di Giorgio. The guitar (its neck suddenly rose before
me like a ladder) had the special addition of a twentieth
fret. This allowed the guitarist to deliver an exquisite high
C on the first string. The piece was sweet and mournful and
swathed – sheathed – *swooning* – with tremolo.

Oh I wish I could stop talking like this!
I wish I could just...
Just rein it in a little.
But the more the words come – the more they flow – the more
I am compelled to feel. And then the words resurface again –
and then the feelings – and then the words – and then the
feelings – in a constantly escalating and self-perpetuating
cycle.

The guitar neck rose before me and I began to climb it like a
ladder, placing my feet carefully on to the individual frets.

D *sharp*
D
C *sharp*
C
B
A *sharp*

I encouraged the little girl to follow on behind me. Mira B
held the ladder firm as we ascended. But when we were
halfway up I realised that the little girl had misplaced her
doll – her baby – her doll. Remember? The baby? Where had
it gone? Who had taken it? Mira B waved her hand at me,
actively encouraging me to continue my ascent. *We are the*
doll, she called, her voice almost obliterated by the trill of
notes – *We are the baby – you and me: Mira A and Mira B.*

What could she mean? My hands suddenly began to
sweat. I lost concentration. The song began to lose its course.

Soon the ladder started wobbling. The little girl froze and clung on tightly. Down below I could see Mira B surrounded by the press. They were snatching at her, nudging her, pulling at her clothing. I reached my hand down to the girl. The strings on the guitar were now vibrating quite violently. I grabbed her hand. I looked up. I began to ascend again more purposefully. The tune was quite deafening. Something at first so poignant, so fleeting, so lovely, had now become angry and threatening and discordant. I thought I might fall, but I held on. The ladder continued to wobble. I dared not look down to discover the fate of Mira B. I just clung on to the girl. I glanced up. I was on the sixteenth fret. What lay above? Just thick smog. I looked straight ahead of me and saw that I had drawn adjacent to a window (in the hospital building). I could see through the window and into a room beyond. There was an operating table, and a surgeon in green scrubs. There were three nurses. And standing close by was an old woman – The Grandmother. Her hands covered her face. Her shoulders rose and fell as she sobbed. I glanced over at the operating table. It was there I saw the small outline of the girl, lying on her back, her arms splayed out, palms raised, her child's belly terrifyingly distended. I tightened my grip on her fingers, but my hand simply formed into a fist. She was gone. I had lost hold of her.

I pushed my face in closer to the window. I tried to call her name but I did not know it. The surgeon – with admirable precision – began to apply his blade to the child's belly. He sliced her open. Then he dug his hand into the hole and withdrew a bag, which he carelessly opened. He tipped the contents down on to the linoleum tiles. One hundred stones.

Next he withdrew a special dog harness. After that a kora. Then a Neuro-Mechanical canine. Then he took out a series of words.

devastated

rotten

abducted

Krishna

Finally he withdrew a gap. A white space. It floated above his hands like a pale cloud and then turned into a dove and flew around the room. It was frantic. It slammed into the window. On the pane, after impact, was left the exquisite, ghostly imprint of its feathers.

I felt a strong urge to open the window. I could not. So I smashed at it with my fist. The glass shattered. I slammed my hand into the hole, knocking out chips and shards. I could feel no pain. The dove flew towards the hole (I ducked) and it escaped. I turned to watch its progress. It flew upwards. Into the smog. And it was then, as I watched it, that I saw ****. I was on the sixteenth fret. **** was standing on the twentieth. He held out his hand to me. I hesitated, and then I stretched out my hand to him. My hand was covered in blood. **** grabbed ahold of my wrist and yanked me up.

We were standing in my room. **** went to my printer and asked for a mesh Wound Healer. Once it had printed he wrapped it, carefully, around my fist.

I should wake up, I thought. But before I did – before I could – I saw another person – a second person – sitting quietly in the corner of the room. In fact I did not see him. At first I *smelled* him. The strangest aroma. Something so alien. I could not quite tell if it was attractive or repulsive. I knew that the smell was *life*. I knew that the smell was *age*.

It was decay.
Death.

**** was talking. He was introducing The Stranger to me.

'Mira A, please, *please* pay attention. I have brought someone to meet you. This is Savannah,' he said.

17

Awake.

**** had disconnected his Graph and his Sensor. Mine still flashed and oscillated. But it was incoherent. It posed no danger. They talked quietly between themselves – **** and The Stranger – almost as if I was not present.

'She has become obliterated by words,' Kite told The Stranger. The Stranger was standing up now. He was moving towards me. He was without embellishments (no Sensor, no Stream) and so he was inexplicable to me. He was holding out his hand. His skin was dark. He was dark. His clothes were dark. There were strange marks on his arms and on his neck. Blueish-black scratches. There was a little teardrop (and a little cross, just beneath it), carefully etched on to his left cheek, under his left eye. The smell of him prickled in my nostrils. It made me feel – it made me feel . . .

It made me feel.

I did not have the language.

Alive?

Lost?

Terrified?

All these words, these *words*. How might I possibly hope to corral them?

I shrank from his touch. I had expected the intelligent fabrics to protect me but their response was surprisingly sluggish.

'She is faded,' The Stranger said, still reaching.

'Am I awake?' I asked. My voice was very quiet.

'Do you hear what she's saying?' **** asked.

'She wants to know if she is awake,' The Stranger told him.

'You are awake.' **** nodded.

'Can you hear me?' I asked The Stranger.

'Perfectly.' The Stranger smiled. His teeth were yellowed. He took my hand and unwound the mesh Wound Repair. His hands were warm. His touch was gentle. He inspected the cuts.

'I love to watch them heal,' he murmured. His eyes were glowing.

'Don't touch her,' **** cautioned sharply. 'You may infect her with something. She is Pure. All is not yet lost. Her future is still In The Balance.'

In *The* Balance?

I was once In Balance.

Am I now In *The* Balance?

How curious that with the addition of merely one, small word – the definite article – everything is transformed. Everything is changed. Everything is undermined.

'She's becoming more and more difficult to decipher,' **** said. 'She is being consumed by narrative. She is making inappropriate connections. She is at once declaring war on The System and becoming synonymous with it. Overlaid by it. Obliterated. The oscillation is the key, I think. She is becoming dangerous to us. There must have been a flaw – a chink.'

'You put the flaw into me,' I whispered hoarsely.

The Stranger tipped his head, frowning.

'What did she just say?' **** asked.

'She says she feels cold,' The Stranger lied.

'Who are you?' I asked, snatching my hand away, then gasping at a curious sensation. A sharp feeling. A vicious heat. Something extreme and quite alien – and yet…yet somehow also oddly familiar – comforting…

Pain?

'I am The Intermediary,' he said.

'Her self has become split between her sense of restraint – of resignation – and her feelings of desire,' **** observed. 'She is a musician.'

'Ah. Like the other girl.' The Stranger nodded. 'They are especially susceptible it would seem.'

'Yes, Tuesday,' **** nodded. 'Although Tuesday was a perfectionist, a fascist. How is she faring?'

'She has established a small niche for herself.' The Stranger smiled. 'She is tough. Her mind is like a closed trap. Eventually – in time – it will consume itself.'

'I don't understand...' I whispered, registering the throb in my hand and peering over towards the window. There was a hole in it. And there was blood on the floor below. The window was healing itself, but slowly, just as my hand was. The carpet was cleaning itself, but slowly, just as the window was. The fibres repelled and then consumed the organic matter that sat red-blackly upon them.

'She is slow to heal,' **** said. 'The narratives are creating conflict in her at a cellular level. She is stressed. She has lost hope.'

'*The tuning fork is in my heart*,' I announced.

'Embedded there, perhaps' – The Stranger chuckled – 'like a knife.'

I was unfamiliar with the language he now spoke. I glanced over towards my Sensor but it simply vibrated with a dense green static – as if a strange mould, or a pondweed – had finally overrun it.

'What is this language?' I asked, intrigued to find myself clumsily speaking it.

'Guaraní,' he murmured. 'We generally like to use it because your Sensors find it difficult to interpret. Many of the words have dual meanings. It is incoherent – contradictory. Your System will not allow for variations. It is rigid.

If you understand me then you must have visited our Holy Place, because for our people words are souls.'

'What are you saying?' **** asked impatiently, plainly now feeling the lack of his Sensor.

'She has visited our Holy Place,' The Stranger said.

'A Cathedral.' **** nodded, signally unimpressed. 'There is a musician – 91.51.9.81.81.1.2–14.9.02.91.12.7.1 – who composed a piece of music by that title: *The Cathedral*. This is what initially led her astray, we feel. Then the idea became embedded. There is a fluctuation in the metal strings he played on. A special vibration. There was a sister star of the same name as hers which oscillated. Something fused. Something random and meaningless. But she has used narrative to construct a story and now the Stream is pounding her with related, yet completely arbitrary information.'

'I am Imperfect,' I murmured. 'There was an oscillation in my Oracular Devices. They implanted something into me. The System is not Pure, it is corrupted. I am becoming The System because – like it – I am impure.'

After I stopped speaking I started.

What was I saying?

What was I thinking?

Could this even be me speaking?

Truly?

Wasn't it . . . wasn't it perhaps only *her*?

'Listen,' The Stranger murmured, 'if you've seen the shapes, the gaps, the whiteness, then you are in serious jeopardy. When **** discovers this you will be cast out. If you want to save yourself then you need to believe in The System again.

By an act of will. In simply believing you shall eventually become Pure.'

'What are you saying?' **** was growing enraged now.

'I am speaking to her in Spanish,' The Stranger lied. 'She seems to follow the occasional word.'

He turned to me again. 'You do not want to enter The Unknown. It is a world of confusion. Your clamps will be rejected by your body out there. We do not have medicine like The Young. You are better off staying here. Compromise. Adapt. Save yourself. Close everything down while you still can.'

I gazed at him, in silence.

'I know that piece.' The Stranger – Savannah – nodded towards ****, but his eyes remained fixed on me. 'There are three parts to it. The Prelude was written long after the other two movements, but now it sits at the start. It is wistful, melancholy. There are bells ringing throughout. And an organ plays Bach. The composer – Agustín Barrios – was of indigenous blood. A great Romantic. A genius.'

'He died, in poverty, of syphilis,' **** sneered. 'What possible romance is there in that?'

'I can't expect you to understand why this resonates with us so deeply.' The Stranger laughed. 'You are Perfected, and we, as you know, are anything but Perfect.'

'Well now you have seen her' – **** indicated towards me with a dismissive sneer – 'do you think you will be able to create a livable space for her on your territory?'

'There is plague' – The Stranger shrugged – 'and turmoil and hunger. But I am sure it is possible, nonetheless.'

'Can you reason with her?' **** wondered. 'I have tried

and failed. Another of her friends – a Youth called Kipp – has also attempted, but to no avail. Perhaps you can make her understand how life is death in your world, how faith is war. How words are fluid. How freedom kills certainty. How narrative pervades every tiny chink and crack and orifice and poisons everything.'

The Stranger returned his eyes to me once again. 'I think she already knows,' he murmured.

'Do you love The Young?' he asked.

As he said the word 'love' I felt it change on his tongue. This was his language. Where nothing was static.

'I can't answer your question,' I said. 'It fluctuates.'

'There is no Certainty in The Unknown.' He nodded. 'But you may find Certainty here, if you choose to.'

'What are you saying?' **** asked, irritated.

'I am explaining to her that in my world there is chaos…' He paused. 'Those clamps in her head are very large. What possible purpose are they serving?'

'They have mechanised selective parts of her brain.' **** shrugged. 'To try and correct the flaw.'

'This explains why Tuesday was attracted to her.' The Stranger nodded. 'But it will make it harder for her to express herself emotionally. That will be challenging, surely, for a musician?'

'Sometimes it is necessary,' **** sighed. 'The line between what is human and what is perfect is an intangible one.'

The Stranger scowled. Then he turned to me and whispered:

'*I KNOW THAT THE ROCK IS ROCK, AND THAT THE WATER OF*

THE RIVER

221

FLEES FROM YOUR STARTLED WAIST, AND THAT THE BIRDS
USE THE LOFTY REFUGE OF THE HUMILIATED TREE
AS A PRECIPICE FOR THEIR SONG AND THEIR WINGS . . .

YOU ARE WITHIN ME WITH ALL YOUR BANNERS;
WITH YOUR LABOURER'S HONEST HANDS,
AND YOUR SMALL, IRREMEDIABLE MOON . . .'

I did not understand his meaning, but my heart palpitated. It felt squeezed and released in one instant.

'What did you say to her?' **** asked.

'I told her to be careful,' The Stranger said, 'not to be seduced by language. It can often be beguiling – seductive – beautiful, yet it is also unpredictable, dangerous, even lethal.'

Shortly afterwards, they left together.
My hand was now almost healed. And the carpet was clean. And the window. I walked over to stand beside it.
My Sensor suddenly flashed:

'IRREMEDIABLE' it barked, pinkening. 'Definition: IMPOSSIBLE TO CURE OR PUT RIGHT.'

My eye lifted to a point just above where the window had been restored. There was a mark remaining. The imprint of a bird. Its feathers etched in a light, whitish grease. Its wing, its neck, its chest.

How might that be possible? I wondered. I glanced around

the room for the dog, Tuck. There was no sign of him. His basket, his toys, everything was gone.

As if he had never been there in the first place.

Turn away, Mira A, I murmured, pushing all thoughts of this from my mind.

Let it go, Mira A. Let it go. Turn away. Turn away. Turn away.

18

A brief study of Mira A.

This written account of Mira A's activities has been downloaded directly from her Information Stream and then mechanically filtered.

This written account of Mira A's activities is available to everyone.

This written account of Mira A's activities has been automatically edited to improve legibility and avoid unnecessary repetition.

The particular time-frame has been specifically requested.

All the above information will, as a matter of course, be forwarded to Mira A herself.

Everything is Open.
Everything is Pure.
Everything is Clean.

Mira A is working diligently. Mira A's Graph has not greened or purpled now for many weeks. Mira A asks no questions. Mira A's skin-tone is much more healthy-looking. Mira A is no longer faded. Mira A exudes a quiet radiance. Mira A's clamps are now fully embedded. Every morning Mira A runs for fifteen minutes on her Power Spot. The energy Mira A generates she applies to altruistic causes.

Mira A is eating sensibly. Mira A sleeps peacefully at night. Mira A actively seeks out the dreams provided by The System and follows them readily.

Mira A seems H A P P Y. Mira A is H A P P Y.

Mira A is Whole. Mira A is Complete. Mira A is In Balance.

Several tests have been set for Mira A and Mira A has passed them all.

If Mira A's Stream fluctuates – as it sometimes does, because there is a flaw – Mira A sits quietly and waits for the fluctuation to pass. Mira A has taken to occupying herself with mechanical puzzles. Mira A seems to find an increased level of satisfaction in them.

Mira A has lost all interest in traditional forms of music. Mira A no longer plays her guitar. Mira A has taken up a new hobby.

In detail:

Several days after Mira A forced her hand through her window, Mira A could be found sitting idly at her table. Mira A's thoughts were as follows:

I wonder...?
No. Turn away.

But do...?
No. Turn away.

But did **** actually...?
No. Turn away.

Turn away, Mira A. Stay Pure. Stay innocent. Live in This Moment. Yes. Here. In This Moment.

The tuning fork is...
The tuning fork...

Uh...

Mira A's eyes suddenly scan the room. Mira A stands up. Mira A walks over to her kora case. Mira A opens it. Mira A removes the kora from within the case.

How can I rest, Mira A murmurs, astonished, when the kora is still...still imperfect?

Mira A begins to pull at the leather rings that have been affixed to the kora's neck. One by one Mira A carefully removes them. Mira A hunts around in the bottom of the kora case for the original, perfected kora pegs. Mira A carefully screws the original, perfected kora pegs back into place again and gently attaches the individual strings to them.

Mira A sits quietly and breathes deeply. Then Mira A locates her A chord 440Hz tuning fork and softly strikes it. Mira A commences retuning the kora. Mira A spends almost an hour trying to retune the kora, but for some reason Mira A seems incapable of finding satisfaction in the sound of the notes. Every so often Mira

A strikes the tuning fork on her knee, lifts the tuning fork to her ear and listens to it gently resonating. Mira A frowns.

The following day, Mira A returns to the kora once again. Mira A tries to retune the kora. Every so often Mira A murmurs:

The tuning fork is in your...

The tuning fork is...
The tuning...

Then Mira A scowls. Mira A strikes her A chord 440Hz tuning fork on her knee and hums the sound it produces gently under her breath. Mira A repeats this process several times but on the last strike Mira A hums at a slightly different pitch to the A chord 440Hz fork. Several times Mira A checks her Sensor to see if the A chord 440Hz tuning fork is sounding accurately. Mira A's Sensor confirms that it is. Mira A has spent almost an hour sounding the A chord 440Hz tuning fork. It is now time for Mira A to attend a lecture on Clouds which she has been keenly anticipating for several weeks.

After Mira A's lecture on Clouds (gaze here for attendance figures, mean temperature, general reception etc.) Mira A returns to her room where – rather than eating a small meal, which her Graph tells her she is in need of – Mira A goes over to her printer and painstakingly produces a new A chord 440Hz tuning fork. But this fork is at 435Hz. After the printer has produced Mira A's new fork, Mira A takes it and sits down with the kora and sounds it. Once again Mira A commences an attempt at retuning the kora. Once again Mira A fails. The following day Mira A returns to the kora, but she appears to have lost all interest in the instrument now. Instead Mira A's attention is focused entirely on her new 435Hz tuning fork. Mira A strikes it and listens to it carefully. Mira A frowns. Mira A places it aside. Mira A returns to her printer and checks its Resource Levels. Low. Mira A grimaces. Mira A walks over to her Power Spot and commences running on it. Mira A runs on her Power Spot for the best part of an hour. Mira A then waits for ten minutes, drinks a glass of water and eats a very small meal. After eating, Mira A lies down for fifteen minutes. Mira A's thoughts are as follows:

Will there be...?

Don't ask.

But have I done enough to...?

It's immaterial. Turn away.

Oh. If I could only...

Live here. Now. In This Moment, Mira A. Don't be led by desire.

Mira A suddenly lifts her left hand and softly touches the knuckles of her right hand with her fingertips. Mira A lifts up her right hand and inspects how well it has healed since...since... Mira A thinks:

Barely a scar.

Then her consciousness is permeated with the scent of . . .

Old sweat

Mira A shudders. Her eyes turn to the window. Mira A sits up. She grabs the coverlet from her bed, walks over to the window and painstakingly polishes all the individual panes of glass with it. Mira A inspects the window and then carefully polishes it for a second time. Mira A returns the coverlet to her bed. The coverlet has self-cleaned before Mira A's even had the chance to spread it out again. The coverlet is Perfect. Mira A murmurs:

Pristine

This word pinkens slightly – just very slightly – on Mira A's Graph. Mira A scowls.

Turn away . . . Mira A mutters.

Turn away, Mira A.

Mira A goes to sit at her table and starts to try and solve a new puzzle, but after only a few minutes Mira A places the puzzle down and returns to her printer. Mira A inspects the Resource Levels. Low/Medium.

Mira A thinks hard for a minute and then starts to instruct the Printer. Mira A pauses, mid-way. Mira A reconsiders. Mira A offers a new set of instructions. As Mira A offers them – and as the Printer accepts them – Mira A is startled to notice her Information Screen – her Graph – her Sensor – all beginning to oscillate.

Mira A goes to sit down. Mira A closes her eyes for a moment. Mira A opens her eyes again. Mira A quietly sits the oscillation out. Mira A does not look at her Information Screen as a series of words jump and spiral around on it. Mira A just stares towards the window, blankly.

I am Innocent.
I am Clean and Unencumbered.
I have been released from The Past – from the Tight Bonds of History.

After several minutes the oscillation passes. Mira A inhales several times in quick succession. Mira A picks up her puzzle again. Mira A spends the next thirty-seven minutes and thirty-five seconds concentrating on her puzzle.

Once the puzzle has been completed, Mira A places it down gently on the table and gets up to go and inspect her printer. A tuning fork has been produced. Mira A picks up the tuning fork. The tuning fork strikes an A chord at 432Hz. Mira A strikes the fork. The fork resonates. Mira A listens to the resonating 432Hz A chord tuning fork and quietly nods, then slowly begins to smile.

An hour passes. During this time Mira A sounds the fork over and over again. Mira A conducts a series of experiments with the fork. Mira A holds it at different angles to her head and to her body. Mira A touches either end of the vibrating fork to random segments of her torso. Mira A places the resonating fork in a glass of water, studies the water for a while and then drinks some of it. Mira A repeats this process for a second time and then uses the remaining liquid on a small orchid she has planted in a pot on her windowsill. Finally, Mira A sits quietly, in her chair, her eyes closed, sounds the 432Hz fork and listens to it, apparently searching for a similar resonance within her own body. As Mira A does this her Sensor becomes...

Temporary Loss of Transmission.

I am not speaking. There are no words, as such. I am simply vibrating. It is not wrong – surely? It is not illicit. It is just a quiet oscillation. A call and response. A little earlier, while I was printing up the 432Hz tuning fork, when my Stream began spewing out information, I turned away from it (as I had determined to do). I looked towards the window – newly polished and clean – a marker, surely, of all my good intentions? And then, as I gazed over there, I noticed that the Stream was reflecting into the shining window pane. The Stream was flashing, in green. A number and two digits:

Then it said:

Schumann Resonance. 1952. The vibration of the planet.
A global electromagnetic resonance originating in the
electrical discharges of lightning between the earth and
the ionosphere:

8Hz.

When both hemispheres of the human brain are synchronised
with each other at –

8Hz

they operate in much greater harmony and experience a
more productive exchange of information.

There then followed an illustration – which rapidly oscillated – of a circle (possibly an egg) that had been divided in half:

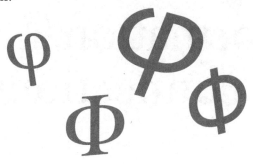

An egg divided, I mused – split in half – like the two hemi-spheres of the brain, or like when twins are conceived, I thought –
A and B

'...the first soul is called the egg...'

The Sensor kept on spewing out information, possibly spurred on by my musings:

Stop thinking, Mira A! Stop thinking! Stop thinking!

'...Then comes the little soul, located in the centre. Completely surrounding the egg is the shell or hide: the *vatjeche*...'

My Graph began flashing:

This is random information. All connections

are arbitrary.
There is no
overall
plan.
This is random
information.
There is no unity
here.
All unity is in
The System.
This is random

information.
Any attempt
to form these
random facts into
a narrative will
meet with chaos.
All Order, all Unity,
all Purity is encoded
into The System.
This is random
information…

I drew a deep breath and returned my attention to the puzzle as it lay before me on the table. I tried not to think. I tried not to feel.

I am Innocent.

I am Clean and Unencumbered.

I have been released from The Past – from the Tight Bonds of History.

Yes. These were my thoughts. But they did not feel like my thoughts. They felt mechanical. They felt...they felt flat – unreal. But I completed the puzzle. I even took some satisfaction in it. Then, when everything was quiet again, when the oscillation had abated, I walked over to my printer. I gazed down at the new tuning fork. I reached out my hand and I picked it up. I held it. Then I struck it.

Oh, the pleasure it afforded my ears! The ring of it! The tone! The resonance! So perfect! So right! So whole! I struck it again and again and again and again. I didn't think. I just heard. I just... I just *felt*. Until eventually just hearing it, just feeling it, didn't seem quite enough. I now longed to enter the vibration utterly, completely. So I sat down quietly and I tried to find an answer within myself. I tried to find my own response. I walked around inside the darkness of my mind, searching for it, hunting for it. I crouched in a corner of my eardrum and held my breath. I listened. I waited for the throb. And then, when I had almost given up hope, it sounded (but very slightly, very vaguely). Had I simply imagined it? I listened again. I knew that the vibration couldn't be heard only once – it was a vibration, after all, it would ring and echo, it would pulse and quake, because it was *alive*. So I listened . . . I listened, and, after a brief interval, I heard it again. And I called it to me. And it came, uncertain at first, nervously, but soon, with increasing confidence, in gentle ripples, and then in waves, lapping against the edges of my consciousness.

I opened my eyes. I don't know why. Perhaps to try and see if I could keep the vibration humming even when I was fully sentient, but as I opened my eyes I saw that the oscillation had returned to my Sensor, my Graph, my Stream, and with it, a slew of information, disgorging itself with greater and greater urgency, with greater and greater levels of pinkening and purpling:

JUST INTONATION

– The Sensor barked – = PURE INTERVALS BETWEEN EACH NOTE, MATHEMATICALLY RELATED BY RATIOS OF SMALL WHOLE NUMBERS. TWELVE-TONE EQUAL TEMPERAMENT = UNIVERSALLY ADOPTED IN 18 . . . IN 18 . . . IN 1953 . . . IN 18 . . . IN 1953 . . . MISTUNES ALL CONSONANT INTERVALS EXCEPT THE OCTAVE.

And then it sang – it literally began to sing – in a new harmony:

In order that the slaves might resound the wonders of your creations with loosened vocal cords, Wash the guilt from our polluted lips...
Saint John.

Ut queant laxis Resonare fibris
Mira gestorum Famuli tuorum
Solve polluti Labii reatum

The Sensor now began to produce an extraordinary variety of different tunings – in the chord of A – a selection of possibilities – and whenever the 432Hz tuning was sounded, a vibration would fill the air, and bounce from –

 Ut to

Re to

Mi to

Fa to

Sol to

La

New tunings – different frequencies – pure sound. And as they played:

8Hz

would begin to resonate, like a powerful jet of water at the heart of a giant fountain, and all the other notes would cascade from it, forming themselves into a sequence of inexplicable numbers and equations and symbols, sometimes interrupted by explanatory headings, and sometimes not –

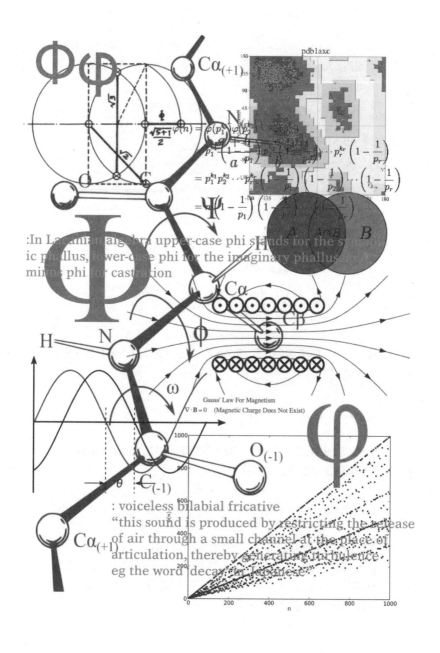

pdb1axc

:In Lacanian algebra upper-case phi stands for the symbolic phallus, lower-case phi for the imaginary phallus, and minus phi for castration

A $A \cap B$ B

Gauss' Law For Magnetism
$\nabla \cdot \mathbf{B} = 0$ (Magnetic Charge Does Not Exist)

: voiceless bilabial fricative
"this sound is produced by restricting the release of air through a small channel at the place of articulation, thereby generating turbulence. eg the word 'decay' in Japanese"

In Lacanian algebra upper-case phi stands for the *symbolic* phallus, lower-case phi for the *imaginary* phallus, and minus phi for castration

A = THE BIG OTHER

D = DEMAND

D = DESIRE

E = THE STATEMENT

E = THE ENUNCIATION

M = THE EGO

S = THE SYMBOLIC ORDER

R = THE FIELD OF REALITY

V = THE WILL TO ENJOY

WE ARE THE POSITIVE AND THE NEGATIVE POLES – A AND B!

A voice suddenly whispered –

THE SYSTEM WANTS TO CONTROL YOU WITH ITS IRRATIONAL TUNING!

It warned:

THE SYSTEM IS DISCORDANT! IT IS NOT PURE! ITS TUNING IS NOT PURE! ITS 440HZ TUNING IS IRRATIONAL! IT CANNOT CORRESPOND TO THE BEAT OF THE PLANET

THEY ARE AFRAID OF TRUE CLARITY!

8Hz.

LISTEN!

8Hz.

THIS IS YOUR OSCILLATION! THEY HAVE TRIED TO
DESTROY IT WITH THEIR SURGERIES AND THEIR
CLAMPS, BUT YOU HAVE FOUND IT ANYWAY, IN SPITE
OF THEIR BEST EFFORTS!

Who are you?
I demanded.

YOU KNOW WHO I AM. I AM THE NEGATIVE POLE.
I AM THE SECOND STAR. WE HAVE BEEN REUNITED
BY PHI – BY THE

8Hz RESONANCE. I AM YOUR DESIRE.

'My desire,' I whispered, 'is to turn away from these thoughts. My…my…'

8Hz.

LISTEN!

8Hz THE FREQUENCY OF THE DOUBLE
HELIX IN DNA REPLICATION. WE ARE TWO. WE ARE ONE!

I must not indulge this voice, I told myself firmly. This voice is just another, random part of the narrative that I have invented – I don't know why – to tell the wrong story of myself. I must turn away from this voice. I must turn away from it.

But the oscillation was very deep now. Furniture was starting to move about. The walls shook.

This is random
information.
All connections are
arbitrary.
There is no overall
plan.
This is random
information.
There is no unity here.
All unity is in
The System.
This is random
information.

Any attempt to form these random facts into a narrative will meet with chaos.
All Order, all Unity, all Purity is encoded into The System. This is random information…

The Graph, The Sensor, all tried to call out. But the fountain of notes and equations were filling the room. Even the voice of Mira B was now losing its clarity.

What should I do?
Reject the resonance? But it was fully embedded – vibrating off the new clamps, flying back and forth between them at an inconceivable speed.
I was helpless! I did not know if there was anything I *could* do…even if I felt the…felt the…the *desire*.
I closed my eyes. It was here I saw ****, standing in front of me.

'I gave you another chance,' he hissed, 'and this is how you choose to repay my generosity? With a destructive resonance?'

'Everything is shaking itself apart!' I gasped.

'You created the tuning fork!' he yelled. 'This is *your* doing!'

'The tuning fork is in my heart!' I exclaimed. 'There was nothing vindictive in it! You sent me to the Kora Group. You told me about The Cathedral. You said there was another star – a sister star that oscillated! You created the neural pathways! This is not my fault!'

Kite was not listening. He could not hear me. He was trying to find some measure of stability within my mind, because there was oscillation, and the equations were trying to force their way between my eyelids. They were trying to prise them open.

**** pointed to his own Sensor, which was working, behind him, but oscillating:

This is

random information.

All

connections

are arbitrary.
There is no
overall
plan.
This is
random

information.
There is no
unity
here.
All

unity is

in

The System.

This is

random

information.

Any attempt to

form these

random facts into a

narrative will meet

with chaos.

All Order,

all

Unity,

all Purity is

encoded...

YOU HAVE

DECLARED

WAR ON THE

SYSTEM!

YOU HAVE

DECLARED WAR ON THE SYSTEM! YOU HAVE DECLARED WAR ON THE SYSTEM!

**** shrieked.

I opened my eyes and then quickly closed them. The room was collapsing. The world was in free-fall. I could not stop the resonance. It had synchronised the two parts of my brain. I was destroying everything. I closed my eyes again. My head was full of equations, scoring off each other, bouncing off each other, generating each other, devouring each other, forming into spirals and stars and patterns. Where could I go? Where was my refuge? Not in The System. I had declared war on The System! I had declared war on The Young! Or at least the narrative – with all its words and words and words and words and words and words...

I started to cry. Everything was lost. And then, out of the chaos I suddenly heard a...did I? Could I? Yes. *Yes*. I heard a waltz. But far away, hidden deep within the blare, the cacophony. It was lost in the margins. On the edge of the page. And it was her tune. It was *her* tune. So I focused all my energy upon it: *one* two three, *one* two three, *one* two three...Everything I had, I focused upon it. And in that instant, without any jarring or confusion, in a billion tiny calculations, in the infinite squiggle of a bottomless cauldron of seething black ants, I suddenly built it (it built itself). I saw it forming – arching up with a terrifying grandeur and solidity out of all of the quaking and the chaos and the confusion. I built it! *We* built it – she built it with me, surely? Because there it stood: Our hope. Our shelter. Our refuge.

Towering above us.
Dark. Ancient. Remorseless.
Terrifying:

The Cathedral.

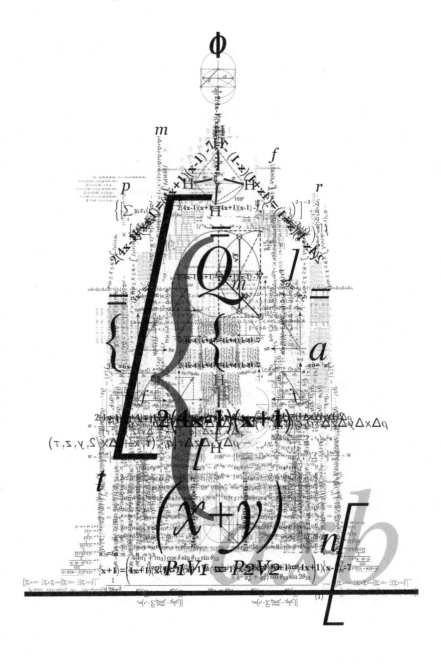

19
The Sacrifice.

It's so quiet – so very still. I can hear my own breath. Every-thing (all that heady, violent, ecstatic reverberation – and even the sweet, lilting waltz that somehow contrived to bring me here) is obliterated by the giant, dark walls. Perhaps it is the architecture? Perhaps the huge arches within the main body of the building suck all the vibrations upwards and trap them in the rafters?

I glance around. Am I alone? For some reason I peer behind me, towards the entrance, squinting in the half-light. I am standing in the foyer. There is someone by the door – remember? The person by the door? The huge, oak door, which is half ajar? But they cannot come in. They are unable to enter. I look down at myself, and am shocked to see that I am very young – small – eight, nine years of age, and my belly is massively distended. I place my child's hands upon my belly, almost in wonder, and it throbs under my touch. Everything throbs. Am I truly nothing more than a million shuddering after-shocks?

The resonances start to bubble up. But I am strong. I turn away. I turn away from them. The Young – The System – have taught me this, at least.

Turn away! Turn away, Mira A!

I quickly pivot and peer towards the door again. I feel a strong urge to go and see who is standing in the shadows there. I sniff the air. I sense danger – darkness. I smell – musk. Yes. I smell – dirt. I smell – corruption. I smell – *life*. I smell – death. Yes. Death.

I know that aroma so well. It is familiar. Is it … is it him? The Stranger? The Intermediary? My heart flutters.

The organ starts to play Bach. I pronounce the name with ease. *Bach*. No numbers in this black Cathedral – because this is my narrative – no masonry, no bricks, no judgement, just sound. Just words.

The piece being performed is *The Well-Tempered Clavier*. It is beautiful, but lonely. I glance towards my Sensor. My Sensor tells me that this piece of music has been composed with Equal Tuning. It is therefore irrational – discordant. Compromised. But then it flashes up another message:

THERE IS *NO CONSPIRACY*! NO CONSPIRACY OF TUNING AND SOUND! THIS IS MERELY A NARRATIVE – *YOUR* NARRATIVE. THIS IS JUST CIRCULAR LOGIC. AND *IT* IS IRRATIONAL!

I scowl and quickly walk forward – as if to escape my Sensor (which I have constructed, surely, along with The Cathedral? This is *my* architecture, *my* story, after all). I move swiftly past the rear pews, and suddenly I feel myself losing balance. I have stepped on to something – a marble – a small, round stone? I begin to fall backwards and lunge for the nearest pew to try and save myself, but before I land and crash I am grabbed by a man and firmly righted. He is on his knees beside me, intent on picking up the stones. One hundred stones. He is wearing a beautiful dress suit. His hair is fragrantly oiled. His shoes...as he crawls about, they *squeak.*

It is *him*, surely? This is *his* Cathedral, *his* composition (and the Bach his inspiration, was it not? Its ringing tones? Its tempered harmony? Its austere, sombre authority?).

He gently releases me and then immediately returns to his former task –

TERRIBLE DISCIPLINE!

without even a word, a nod.

('Beloved brother, I have promised Don Luis, before I leave for Paraguay, to give him a pig so his wife, Dona Guillermina, who is very good at preparing pork chorizo sausages...' my Sensor whispers.)

I glance behind him and there I see his other self – his native self – with his wide, indigenous lip, his bare chest, his war-paint, his feathers, his beloved guitar with its metal strings.

'Whose Cathedral is this – mine or yours?' I enquire of the kneeling man (all those tiny stitches on his upper lip, and, on closer inspection, his cheeks so sallow, his eyes so bloodshot).

THIS IS ONLY NARRATIVE! my Sensor flashes. SIMPLY NARRATIVE! NOTHING MORE. THERE IS NOTHING COHERENT HERE, ONLY A SERIES OF SENTENCES CONNECTED BY GRAMMAR. YOU ARE SELECTING CHARACTERS FROM A STORY THAT YOU CONSTRUCT-ED YOURSELF FROM RANDOM COMPONENTS. THERE IS NO HOPE BEYOND THE SYSTEM. THERE IS NO TRUTH BEYOND THE SYSTEM. *KNOW* THIS!

I scowl and turn again to the native – the performer – the patriot – the humiliation – the farce. Which of these two should I address? I wonder. Which do I prefer? Both are unreal. Both have been so carefully, so painstakingly con-structed. Can these two – so different: the one so civilised, so polite, so careful; the other so fearless and ridiculous and romantic – be merely one entity? Is that feasible? How might I conceivably hope to address them when I am not even able to unite them successfully within my own consciousness?

The native Barrios sits down on a pew and begins to play. The kneeling Barrios covers his ears.

WHERE IS THE TRUTH? a familiar voice whispers. LOST SOMEWHERE BETWEEN THE POSITIVE AND THE NEGATIVE POLES? BOUNCING HELPLESSLY BACK AND FORTH BETWEEN TWO OPPOSITES?

Something kicks in my belly.

I cannot answer this question, so I peer deeper into the body of The Cathedral. I am looking for comfort. I am look-ing for the praying people – the kneelers – the ones I'd seen previously, in other dreams. A narrative that demands less of me, perhaps. A narrative of family. And...ah yes, there they are. I hurry towards them. Four figures. Two young girls – my sisters, slightly older than me – and another woman (the instinctive warmth in my heart tells me that she is my mother). I note (with some dismay) that she is wearing prison overalls. And sitting just along from her, a short distance away? The Grandmother I saw previously, weeping in the hospital. I walk towards them, clutching at my belly, calling out. They all turn. They see me. I notice that they are surrounded by boulders, by stones. Dozens of large stones. Hundreds of large stones. Their hands and their clothes are covered in dust. They look hot – exhausted. They cover their faces when they see me. They lean forward. They start to wail and to ululate. They are fearful. They are plaintive. They are ashamed.

'The date of the festival is December 8th, which is, of course, the feast of the Immaculate Conception of the Blessed Virgin...'

my Sensor grumbles, hoarsely,

'...and for weeks beforehand the "promeseros" – or those persons who for various reasons have made vows to pay tribute to the Virgin of Caacupé – start from all parts of the Paraguayan Republic on foot, on horseback or in bullock-carts...and pay substantial tribute to the image of the Virgin as a kind of thank offering for being relieved of their troubles. Even the very poorest of the poor – those who can offer no tribute in money in fulfilment of their vows – will actually carry for many miles a huge stone balanced on their head. And outside the church at Caacupé, which I will show you presently, there are many piles of these extraordinary tokens, some of which weigh as much as thirty pounds…'

'AFTER FIVE OR SIX DAYS, HE BEGAN DRINKING A LITTLE HONEY, DILUTED WITH WATER…'

my Sensor quickly runs on,

'WACHUGI, THE MOTHER OF HIS VICTIM, WAS THE ONE WHO PREPARED IT AND BROUGHT IT TO HIM. SHE TOOK CARE OF HER DAUGHTER'S KILLER AS IF HE WERE HER OWN CHILD, AS THOUGH IN HER EYES JAKUGI NOW HAD TO TAKE THE PLACE OF THE GIRL HE HAD ROBBED HER OF. THIS IS THE WAY IT IS AMONG THE ATCHEI. A MAN KILLS A CHILD OUT OF REVENGE: HE IMMEDIATELY STEPS IN TO FILL THE VOID HE HAS CREATED, HE BECOMES THE MOTHER'S CHAVE AND FROM NOW ON CALLS HER CHUPI-AREGI, MY GODMOTHER. THIS IS WHY SHE FEEDS HIM…WAS THIS ASKING TOO MUCH OF THE MOTHER? IT WAS THE ATCHEI'S RULE. BEYOND THE STRANGE BONDS THAT FORM BETWEEN THE EXECUTIONER AND HIS VICTIM AND CREATE A SECRET SPACE IN WHICH THEY ARE RECONCILED, THERE IS A GUARANTEE IN THE TRIBE THAT THERE WILL BE NO HOSTILITY IN THE TRIBE BETWEEN FAMILIES ASSOCIATED WITH THE SAME MISFORTUNE…'

I am lost for a moment, deep in thought, considering these words – confused by them, perplexed by them – when suddenly I hear a quick movement behind me, beyond the music. I turn and see – to my intense dismay – that it is **** – it is Kite – I can say it now, without fear or anxiety, because this is *my* narrative. And he is advancing upon me, at speed, down the aisle. His tail flies behind him, with its many bows. 'I *indulged* you,' he yells, 'I showed you nothing but tolerance and kindness, and this is how you repay me? By declaring war on The Young? By building this Cathedral? This giant, swarming edifice of contradictory words and empty echoes and meaningless equations?'

HE MEANS TO HARM YOU! Mira B whispers. HE IS THE FLAW. HE WANTS TO DESTROY YOU. HE MEANS TO STOP THE SACRI-FICE. YOU MUST RUN! YOU MUST SAVE YOURSELF! YOU MUST ESCAPE HIM!

'Where will I go?' I gasp. 'I am only small, and my belly is heavy. What is this weight I am carrying?' I demand. 'What is this weight? What shall I call it?'

Sin!

the organ suddenly blasts –

Sin! Sin! Sin! Sin!

FOLLOW! FOLLOW! Mira B calls. She disappears into the gloom. I glance behind me. Kite is approaching. His face is distending. His face is breaking up – as if all the vibration beyond the thick walls of The Cathedral is gradually shaking him into a million tiny fragments.

I follow Mira B along the aisle, past the altar, into the Sacristy, through a succession of dark corridors, until finally we reach the base of a small stairwell. I am out of breath. Mira B climbs the stairs ahead of me.

FOLLOW! FOLLOW! she yells.

I wonder, momentarily, why Mira B's voice has become so much smaller. And all the other voices around me – even that of my Sensor, which is now my voice, is it not? But still, still, I follow her.

The stairwell is small and cramped, and the weight of my belly makes climbing difficult. I twist and I turn and as I ascend I feel the stone walls closing in upon me. But I cannot go back. Kite is following. Kite is behind me. An angry, buzzing swarm of recriminations – a million symbols and numbers and letters hotly pursuing me. At one point – when I stagger on the stairs and rest against the wall for a second – his anger suddenly coheres into a black syringe and its needle injects me. His poison – his remedy – his antidote says:

'The mistake you have made, Mira A, is to think that The Cathedral will set you free! But faith is simply another kind of prison. And from now on your every thought, your every movement, your every impulse, your every yearning, your every word will be subject to an infinitely more savage and restrictive form of censorship than anything The System could ever have dreamed up. Because the censor will be YOU! And the ultimate payoff will not be hopefulness or purity or unity but SIN, but **damnation**! You have built a new prison for yourself, Mira A! And its culmination is pain! Is death!!!'

I continue to climb. Kite's words are an epidural. They have numbed me. And the walls are getting closer. I can barely squeeze my way past them now. They are soft. They are fleshy. And they *throb*. They contract and then release me. It is hard to breathe here. But still I inch my way forward. I inch my way upward. Where is my sister star? Has she been born ahead of me? Or is she here, in my mouth, preparing herself to draw her first breath, to utter her first wail?

The Cathedral labours to give me birth. For a while I am stuck. Will they pull me out with forceps? There is a moment of terrible uncertainty, and then the walls are ripped open and I am plucked out, gasping. I weigh three pounds. I am tiny and naked and innocent. I am unwanted. I am impossible. I am unnatural. I am shameful. I am perfect. I am flawed. Around me the air reverberates with otherworldly howls.

This is the Bell-tower. And I am Mira A. I look down at myself to confirm this fact, then gaze across at the giant bell that shares the tower with me. I am standing on a small platform, a couple of feet of scaffolding. I kneel and then inch my way forward and gaze down from this great height to see The Cathedral far down below me, full of infinite versions of myself. Earlier incarnations. My ancestors. This great assembly – the culmination of one, dreadful violation, one awful mistake. They are all singing, in unison:

In order that the slaves might resound the wonders of your creations with loosened vocal cords, Wash the guilt from our polluted lips...

Ut queant laxis Resonare fibris
Mira gestorum Famuli tuorum
Solve polluti Labii reatum

SOMEONE IS MISSING, Mira B yells.

'Where are you?' I ask, squinting, my eyes scanning the only section of the crowd currently visible to me. Is Mira B down there, hidden among them?

OUR FATHER. THE ONE WHO VIOLATED OUR MOTHER. THE ONE WHO DENIED US. HE IS OUTSIDE THE CATHEDRAL. HE CANNOT ENTER – Mira B bellows.

'I don't understand you,' I murmur, still searching for her – for myself – among the mass of people lying far down below.

'Since colonial times, state and community existed as parallel entities that rarely overlapped,' my Stream coughs. 'One was Spanish-oriented and scripted towards the literate world, the other was Guaraní and directed inward as part of Paraguay's oral heritage...for Guaraní had no words to express key political concepts like "parliament" or "representative democracy"...'

I can't really comprehend this, at first. I start to re-read it.

STOP CREATING DIFFERENT NARRATIVES! Mira B howls. STOP TURNING AWAY, MIRA A! FACE UP TO THIS! ELIMINATE THE FLAW! FORGIVE! PERFECT US! BRING HIM INTO THE CATHEDRAL.

NO ONE HAS SHOWN DEFINITIVELY THAT THE COSMOVISION OF AN ARCHAIC SOCIETY IS BETTER OR WORSE THAN THAT OF A MODERN SOCIETY. IT IS JUST DIFFERENT...' my Stream shudders.

'I don't think I fully understand what is being asked of me,' I murmur.
Mira B tries to speak, to answer, but her voice is now infinitesimal. I wonder whether this is because she is too far away from me (obliterated by song), or whether I have made her far away because I do not *want* to hear her. I draw still closer to the edge of the scaffolding and peer down into the crowds below. It is then that I see the tail – the string and the bows – dangling beside me, into the air, into the drop: *Kite!* He has made it up the staircase! He is birthed! He is here! But he is simply a Kite now. Merely his logo. And even that – as I

watch it, horrified – is shuddering itself into nothing. I wonder why I have allowed him to persist. Because this is my
narrative, is it not? I have created The Cathedral – the congregation – the songs – the tower – the bell. Who might have
created this place if not me? And just as I am pondering this,
the tail – Kite's tail – wraps itself, quickly, ruthlessly, around
my wrist and jerks me forward, yanking me, toppling me,
into thin air.

I snatch for the wooden boards that had supported me
previously. I grab at them with one hand, then with the other.
I swing there, panting, legs kicking into nothing. I peer up at
the giant bell. Etched into its huge, brass side is

8Hz.

I marvel at this as I dangle there.
Will I fall?
I do not want to fall.
But my arms quickly grow tired.
I close my eyes.
Will I pray?
    'Shall I help you?' a deep voice asks.
I open my eyes and glance up (although I do not need to look,
because I can *smell* him. I know who he is. Life. Death. Fam-
ine. Hunger).
    'Shall I help you?' he repeats, smiling, and before I can
answer, he places a boot – a filthy, leather boot crudely fash-
ioned from wood and rank animal skins – upon the fingers
of my one hand. I gasp. I feel

He gently applies his full weight to this foot – to my fingers. I sense the bones in my fingers bend, then snap –

I try to shift my other hand – to protect the first – but this hand he quickly traps under his second boot, and presses down hard upon it.

'**I am holding** you,' he says tenderly. '**You will not fall.**'
   'I don't…I can't…'

'…un…un…understand your words,' I stutter. 'They fluctuate.'
He gazes at me, smiling.

'I can't...' I pant, speaking his language now, 'I can't...'
I feel my denial transforming into an affirmation on my
tongue –

So I close my eyes. I call on the resonance. I hear it sounding
in the Latin hymn the crowd below are singing: 'Wash the
guilt from our polluted lips...' I hum. The Stranger hums
with me, but his frequency is lower. As he sings, as I sing –

– I watch tiny, green spirals of equations peeling from the
walls around me –

'The Fibonacci numbers are a perfect pattern of numbers
that can be translated into pitches...they can be found in
seashells, solar systems, architecture and plants. They can
be found in the human body...' my Stream idly muses.
Then it adds,

'Ultra-high frequencies simulate enhanced fractal growth in plants and
encourage stem dilation for increased fertiliser absorption...'

And finally: 'The ratios of neighbouring Fibonacci numbers, when drawn, show
a spiral like that inside a conch shell. Equal Tuning creates a circle – something closed –
not something open like a spiral...'

As the Stream sighs into silence I watch –

as the numbers thicken and expand and forge themselves, organically, into an ornate hanging vine. Their lushness clings on to me and gently supports me like a precious fruit. Their stems and their leaves encase me and cradle me. They crawl up on to the scaffolding and affix themselves to The Stranger's feet. He starts, yanks off his boots and jumps back. With my broken hands finally released, the plant lowers me – inch by glorious inch – rustling and creaking, on to the floor below. But the greening does not stop here. The vine continues to grow and expand. It spreads over the altar, it teems across the walls, it clings on to the windows. It clambers over the pews, it stops the mouths of the singers and lifts their bodies to the rafters. Its luxuriance – its lushness – becomes increasingly dense and fibrous. It hisses and twitters. This is the jungle of words. This is the wilderness. This is cruel nature: the sustainer, the destroyer. Soon I cannot move. My feet are sealed to the floor by suckers. Tendrils slide over my body. I try to sing, but I cannot hear the resonance. The hiss of growth is too powerful. I had created The Cathedral (had I not?) and now the jungle will devour it. I glance down at my broken fingers. What could I possibly do now? If only I could... I try to form them into the shape of a brush (but they are crushed), they are limp, yet still, I lift my arm up, and into the wall of green around me I etch:

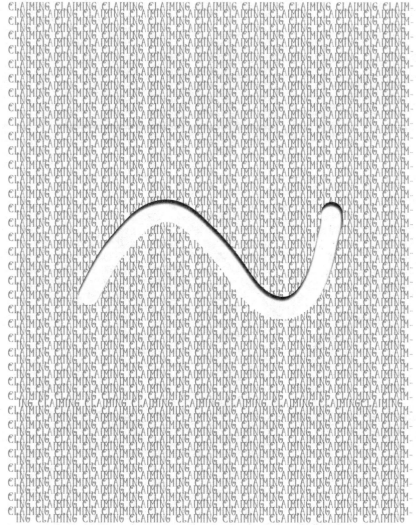

UNKNOWN UNKNOWN UNKNOWN UNKNOWN UNKNOWN UNKNOWN UNKNOWN UNKNOWN

EARTHBOUND SPIRITS EARTHBOUND SPIRITS EARTHBOUND SPIRITS
EARTHBOUND SPIRITS EARTHBOUND SPIRITS EARTHBOUND SPIRITS
EARTHBOUND SPIRITS EARTHBOUND SPIRITS EARTHBOUND SPIRITS
EARTHBOUND SPIRITS EARTHBOUND SPIRITS EARTHBOUND SPIRITS
EARTHBOUND SPIRITS EARTHBOUND SPIRITS EARTHBOUND SPIRITS
EARTHBOUND SPIRITS EARTHBOUND SPIRITS EARTHBOUND SPIRITS
EARTHBOUND SPIRITS EARTHBOUND SPIRITS EARTHBOUND SPIRITS

EARTHBOUND SPIRITS EARTHBOUND SPIRITS EARTHBOUND SPIRITS
EARTHBOUND SPIRITS EARTHBOUND SPIRITS EARTHBOUND SPIRITS
EARTHBOUND SPIRITS EARTHBOUND SPIRITS EARTHBOUND SPIRITS
EARTHBOUND SPIRITS EARTHBOUND SPIRITS EARTHBOUND SPIRITS
EARTHBOUND SPIRITS EARTHBOUND SPIRITS EARTHBOUND SPIRITS
EARTHBOUND SPIRITS EARTHBOUND SPIRITS EARTHBOUND SPIRITS
EARTHBOUND SPIRITS EARTHBOUND SPIRITS EARTHBOUND SPIRITS

PURIFICATION PURIFICATION PURIFICATION PURIFICATION PURIFICATION PURIFICATION
PURIFICATION PURIFICATION PURIFICATION PURIFICATION PURIFICATION PURIFICATION
PURIFICATION PURIFICATION PURIFICATION PURIFICATION PURIFICATION PURIFICATION
PURIFICATION PURIFICATION PURIFICATION PURIFICATION PURIFICATION PURIFICATION
PURIFICATION PURIFICATION PURIFICATION PURIFICATION PURIFICATION PURIFICATION
PURIFICATION PURIFICATION PURIFICATION PURIFICATION PURIFICATION PURIFICATION
PURIFICATION PURIFICATION PURIFICATION PURIFICATION PURIFICATION PURIFICATION
PURIFICATION PURIFICATION PURIFICATION PURIFICATION PURIFICATION PURIFICATION
PURIFICATION PURIFICATION PURIFICATION PURIFICATION PURIFICATION PURIFICATION
PURIFICATION PURIFICATION PURIFICATION PURIFICATION PURIFICATION PURIFICATION
PURIFICATION PURIFICATION PURIFICATION PURIFICATION PURIFICATION PURIFICATION
PURIFICATION PURIFICATION PURIFICATION PURIFICATION PURIFICATION PURIFICATION
PURIFICATION PURIFICATION PURIFICATION PURIFICATION PURIFICATION PURIFICATION
PURIFICATION PURIFICATION PURIFICATION PURIFICATION PURIFICATION PURIFICATION
PURIFICATION PURIFICATION PURIFICATION PURIFICATION PURIFICATION PURIFICATION
PURIFICATION PURIFICATION PURIFICATION PURIFICATION PURIFICATION PURIFICATION
PURIFICATION PURIFICATION PURIFICATION PURIFICATION PURIFICATION PURIFICATION
PURIFICATION PURIFICATION PURIFICATION PURIFICATION PURIFICATION PURIFICATION
PURIFICATION PURIFICATION PURIFICATION PURIFICATION PURIFICATION PURIFICATION
PURIFICATION PURIFICATION PURIFICATION PURIFICATION PURIFICATION PURIFICATION
PURIFICATION PURIFICATION PURIFICATION PURIFICATION PURIFICATION PURIFICATION
PURIFICATION PURIFICATION PURIFICATION PURIFICATION PURIFICATION PURIFICATION
PURIFICATION PURIFICATION PURIFICATION PURIFICATION PURIFICATION PURIFICATION
PURIFICATION PURIFICATION PURIFICATION PURIFICATION PURIFICATION PURIFICATION
PURIFICATION PURIFICATION PURIFICATION PURIFICATION PURIFICATION PURIFICATION
PURIFICATION PURIFICATION PURIFICATION PURIFICATION PURIFICATION PURIFICATION
PURIFICATION PURIFICATION PURIFICATION PURIFICATION PURIFICATION PURIFICATION
PURIFICATION PURIFICATION PURIFICATION PURIFICATION PURIFICATION PURIFICATION
PURIFICATION PURIFICATION PURIFICATION PURIFICATION PURIFICATION PURIFICATION
PURIFICATION PURIFICATION PURIFICATION PURIFICATION PURIFICATION PURIFICATION
PURIFICATION PURIFICATION PURIFICATION PURIFICATION PURIFICATION PURIFICATION
PURIFICATION PURIFICATION PURIFICATION PURIFICATION PURIFICATION PURIFICATION
PURIFICATION PURIFICATION PURIFICATION PURIFICATION PURIFICATION PURIFICATION
PURIFICATION PURIFICATION PURIFICATION PURIFICATION PURIFICATION PURIFICATION
PURIFICATION PURIFICATION PURIFICATION PURIFICATION PURIFICATION PURIFICATION
PURIFICATION PURIFICATION PURIFICATION PURIFICATION PURIFICATION PURIFICATION
PURIFICATION PURIFICATION PURIFICATION PURIFICATION PURIFICATION PURIFICATION
PURIFICATION PURIFICATION PURIFICATION PURIFICATION PURIFICATION PURIFICATION
PURIFICATION PURIFICATION PURIFICATION PURIFICATION PURIFICATION PURIFICATION
PURIFICATION PURIFICATION PURIFICATION PURIFICATION PURIFICATION PURIFICATION
PURIFICATION PURIFICATION PURIFICATION PURIFICATION PURIFICATION PURIFICATION
PURIFICATION PURIFICATION PURIFICATION PURIFICATION PURIFICATION PURIFICATION
PURIFICATION PURIFICATION PURIFICATION PURIFICATION PURIFICATION PURIFICATION
PURIFICATION PURIFICATION PURIFICATION PURIFICATION PURIFICATION PURIFICATION

OTHERS' HEARTS OTHERS' HEARTS OTHERS' HEARTS OTHERS' HEARTS OTHERS' HEARTS
OTHERS' HEARTS OTHERS' HEARTS OTHERS' HEARTS OTHERS' HEARTS OTHERS' HEARTS
OTHERS' HEARTS OTHERS' HEARTS OTHERS' HEARTS OTHERS' HEARTS OTHERS' HEARTS

OTHERS' HEARTS OTHERS' HEARTS OTHERS' HEARTS OTHERS' HEARTS OTHERS' HEARTS
OTHERS' HEARTS OTHERS' HEARTS OTHERS' HEARTS OTHERS' HEARTS OTHERS' HEARTS
OTHERS' HEARTS OTHERS' HEARTS OTHERS' HEARTS OTHERS' HEARTS OTHERS' HEARTS
OTHERS' HEARTS OTHERS' HEARTS OTHERS' HEARTS OTHERS' HEARTS OTHERS' HEARTS

EXORCISM EXORCISM EXORCISM EXORCISM EXORCISM EXORCISM EXORCISM EXORCISM EXORCISM
EXORCISM EXORCISM EXORCISM EXORCISM EXORCISM EXORCISM EXORCISM EXORCISM EXORCISM
EXORCISM EXORCISM EXORCISM EXORCISM EXORCISM EXORCISM EXORCISM EXORCISM EXORCISM
EXORCISM EXORCISM EXORCISM EXORCISM EXORCISM EXORCISM EXORCISM EXORCISM EXORCISM
EXORCISM EXORCISM EXORCISM EXORCISM EXORCISM EXORCISM EXORCISM EXORCISM EXORCISM
EXORCISM EXORCISM EXORCISM EXORCISM EXORCISM EXORCISM EXORCISM EXORCISM EXORCISM
EXORCISM EXORCISM EXORCISM EXORCISM EXORCISM EXORCISM EXORCISM EXORCISM EXORCISM
EXORCISM EXORCISM EXORCISM EXORCISM EXORCISM EXORCISM EXORCISM EXORCISM EXORCISM
EXORCISM EXORCISM EXORCISM EXORCISM EXORCISM EXORCISM EXORCISM EXORCISM EXORCISM
EXORCISM EXORCISM EXORCISM EXORCISM EXORCISM EXORCISM EXORCISM EXORCISM EXORCISM
EXORCISM EXORCISM EXORCISM EXORCISM EXORCISM EXORCISM EXORCISM EXORCISM EXORCISM
EXORCISM EXORCISM EXORCISM EXORCISM EXORCISM EXORCISM EXORCISM EXORCISM EXORCISM
EXORCISM EXORCISM EXORCISM EXORCISM EXORCISM EXORCISM EXORCISM EXORCISM EXORCISM
EXORCISM EXORCISM EXORCISM EXORCISM EXORCISM EXORCISM EXORCISM EXORCISM EXORCISM
EXORCISM EXORCISM EXORCISM EXORCISM EXORCISM EXORCISM EXORCISM EXORCISM EXORCISM
EXORCISM EXORCISM EXORCISM EXORCISM EXORCISM EXORCISM EXORCISM EXORCISM EXORCISM
EXORCISM EXORCISM EXORCISM EXORCISM EXORCISM EXORCISM EXORCISM EXORCISM EXORCISM
EXORCISM EXORCISM EXORCISM EXORCISM EXORCISM EXORCISM EXORCISM EXORCISM EXORCISM
EXORCISM EXORCISM EXORCISM EXORCISM EXORCISM EXORCISM EXORCISM EXORCISM EXORCISM
EXORCISM EXORCISM EXORCISM EXORCISM EXORCISM EXORCISM EXORCISM EXORCISM EXORCISM
EXORCISM EXORCISM EXORCISM EXORCISM EXORCISM EXORCISM EXORCISM EXORCISM EXORCISM
EXORCISM EXORCISM EXORCISM EXORCISM EXORCISM EXORCISM EXORCISM EXORCISM EXORCISM
EXORCISM EXORCISM EXORCISM EXORCISM EXORCISM EXORCISM EXORCISM EXORCISM EXORCISM
EXORCISM EXORCISM EXORCISM EXORCISM EXORCISM EXORCISM EXORCISM EXORCISM EXORCISM
EXORCISM EXORCISM EXORCISM EXORCISM EXORCISM EXORCISM EXORCISM EXORCISM EXORCISM
EXORCISM EXORCISM EXORCISM EXORCISM EXORCISM EXORCISM EXORCISM EXORCISM EXORCISM
EXORCISM EXORCISM EXORCISM EXORCISM EXORCISM EXORCISM EXORCISM EXORCISM EXORCISM
EXORCISM EXORCISM EXORCISM EXORCISM EXORCISM EXORCISM EXORCISM EXORCISM EXORCISM
EXORCISM EXORCISM EXORCISM EXORCISM EXORCISM EXORCISM EXORCISM EXORCISM EXORCISM
EXORCISM EXORCISM EXORCISM EXORCISM EXORCISM EXORCISM EXORCISM EXORCISM EXORCISM
EXORCISM EXORCISM EXORCISM EXORCISM EXORCISM EXORCISM EXORCISM EXORCISM EXORCISM
EXORCISM EXORCISM EXORCISM EXORCISM EXORCISM EXORCISM EXORCISM EXORCISM EXORCISM
EXORCISM EXORCISM EXORCISM EXORCISM EXORCISM EXORCISM EXORCISM EXORCISM EXORCISM
EXORCISM EXORCISM EXORCISM EXORCISM EXORCISM EXORCISM EXORCISM EXORCISM EXORCISM
EXORCISM EXORCISM EXORCISM EXORCISM EXORCISM EXORCISM EXORCISM EXORCISM EXORCISM
EXORCISM EXORCISM EXORCISM EXORCISM EXORCISM EXORCISM EXORCISM EXORCISM EXORCISM
EXORCISM EXORCISM EXORCISM EXORCISM EXORCISM EXORCISM EXORCISM EXORCISM EXORCISM
EXORCISM EXORCISM EXORCISM EXORCISM EXORCISM EXORCISM EXORCISM EXORCISM EXORCISM
EXORCISM EXORCISM EXORCISM EXORCISM EXORCISM EXORCISM EXORCISM EXORCISM EXORCISM
EXORCISM EXORCISM EXORCISM EXORCISM EXORCISM EXORCISM EXORCISM EXORCISM EXORCISM
EXORCISM EXORCISM EXORCISM EXORCISM EXORCISM EXORCISM EXORCISM EXORCISM EXORCISM

DREAMS

I am sweating. This jungle is so...so dense – so unanswerable – it is asphyxiating...the green tendrils – *indestructible, unassailable* – slither up my arms, into the cracks between my ruined fingers.

I am rased. I am demolished. I am *devoured*.

But still – still – I am a voice – a small voice – telling the story of my abrogation. This is nothing, I tell myself, nothing but my own narrative – my own words – and words, surely – I tell myself – are sustained by gaps – by brief interludes – by inhalations.

Do not panic.

Do not panic.

Keep telling the story of yourself. As long as you tell it, Mira A, you cannot be obliterated. Words are souls, are they not?

I create the shapes in my mind, and as I form them the spaces appear ahead of me: the breath of hope fills the aisle. The words of the story shake themselves out. The tendrils release me. I am set free to move forward, into white balloons of air that float in front of me – surrounded by life – but consisting of sacrifice – the space of forgiveness. I am claimed by hope, I step into The Unknown. My earthbound spirit is purified. I seek others' hearts as I walk through the Green Cathedral, towards the entrance. I will keep moving forward, so long as there are words, and I watch them dancing ahead of me, towards the giant door. I am standing at the door and I say

push! push! push!

With each inhale, the exhale.

The giant door swings open.

What lies beyond The Cathedral? I squint out into the darkness. I sense a small commotion, a panting, I feel warm breath on my broken hands. And I hear hooves sounding on the marble floors. Roe bucks. A small herd of them, then more of them and still more of them – a giant herd – moving past me, into The Cathedral; first at a stately walk – nervous, uncertain – and then at a slow trot, then finally a canter.

Above me – in the distance – I hear something shifting. It is the bell – the bell of The Cathedral, inhaling before it sounds. And in that moment, in that inhalation, I see everything teeming into whiteness. In the breath before sound. In the innocence before words. In the hush of possibility.

The bell rings.
The sound engulfs me.

I am obliterated.
I am found.

Where are we? I ask, stirring.

It is dark here. Everything hurts. My body hurts. My mouth is dry. The air around me feels – feels burned.

'Do not worry,' a voice says. I know that voice. It is him – it is Savannah. I peer down through the greasy blear towards his feet. They are bare. The ground is full of broken glass and dirt.

'Have we reached The Unknown?' I ask, quaking. It is…it is *painful* here. I glance around me, horrified. How might I describe this place? What words might I use?

Savannah is collecting tiny shards of wood. He has ripped up part of his rough coat.

'I will make splints for your fingers,' he tells me.

In the distance I hear screams and gunfire. My stomach contracts. What is this feeling?

Hunger?

Everything aches.

'Will my body reject the clamps?' I wonder.

'Give me your hand,' he says, not answering.

I give him my hand. He takes it, gingerly. The fingers are crushed and bloody.

I feel pain.

How might I describe this place?

How might I describe this feeling?

This strangeness?

This fearfulness?

This filth?

This confusion?

This mystery?

This hopefulness?

'Do not try.' He smiles, as if reading my thoughts. 'There is no need.'

I smile back at him. I inhale. I exhale.

Of course. But of course. I softly embrace silence.

Special thanks to Tania Barker for her beautiful artworks, Lindsay Nash for her sterling design input, Anna Argenio for her skill and fortitude, and Peter Lambert and Andrew Nickson for their seminal, scholarly and utterly engrossing *Paraguay Reader* (Duke University Press Books, 2012).